# THE VOICE TEACH[illegible] COOKBOOK

## Creative Recipes for Teachers of Singing

Published by
Meredith Music Publications
a division of G.W. Music, Inc.
1584 Estuary Trail, Delray Beach, FL 33483
http://www.meredithmusic.com



Cover and text design by Shawn Girsberger


First Edition
April 2018

International Standard Book Number: 978-1-57463-476-1
Library of Congress Control Number: 2018936954
Printed and bound in U.S.A.
22 21 20 19 18 PP 1 2 3 4 5

# Contents

# Foreword

Voice science and pedagogy continue to develop and provide new vision of "what's possible" for teachers and singers—much like that of new flavor profiles in cooking! However, for most teachers, finding time to read the latest research and pedagogical applications can be challenging. I liken it to coming home and asking, "What am I going to cook tonight?" Cookbooks provide a "one-stop-shop" of creative ideas and "tried and true" recipes. This book, part of Garwood Whaley's "Cookbook Series for Music Educators," was written for all teachers of singing to provide concise, foundational recipes that expand their current knowledge and pedagogy.

When proposing this book to Gar, I spoke of the challenges facing voice teachers today, and the need for training vocalists to perform multiple styles of music from Renaissance to contemporary pop in an authentic, healthy manner. This book provided the perfect platform to gather and disseminate ideas and strategies from 57 experts from across the U.S. working as professors, studio teachers, professional singers, choral directors, composers, vocologists, and speech-language pathologists. Contributing authors were invited based on their exemplary records of teaching, research, and pedagogical ingenuity. A diverse list of recipe topics was chosen spanning from "Resources for the Voice Studio" to "Using Your Voice as Many Different Sounds" to "Singing Country Vocal Stylisms." Although most topics are unique, some recipes share topics but approach them from an alternative perspective and learning style. Further, since each contributing author is an expert on their recipe topic, readers are encouraged to get their hands dirty and dive deeper into each author's research.

For the beginning voice teacher, I hope these recipes add to your studio philosophy and pedagogy for success in teaching singers. For the future music educator, I hope these recipes inspire you to expand your current knowledge and forge new connections and awareness of possibilities. For the choral conductor and ensemble director, I hope this is a resource for working with individual voices within your ensembles and guiding them outside of the ensemble towards vocal and musical success—many times, you are their only voice teacher. For the expert voice teacher, I hope this book provides you with a resource of experts and stimulates further growth in your professional development and research. For the singer, I hope these recipes provide you with insight into the many facets of voice production, performance, and teaching pedagogy.

The human voice is capable of producing an extraordinary number of vocal sounds. May this cookbook provide insight into the infinite "vocal recipes" that can be produced within many styles of vocal music. Take time to explore each recipe more than once, share your favorites with a colleague, and then develop your own unique recipes based on the fantastic work of each author within this cookbook.

*Find something you're passionate about and keep tremendously interested in it.* — Julia Child

Brian J. Winnie
*Project Coordinator/Editor*

# Acknowledgments

To each of the chefs who contributed to this publication, I offer my sincere thanks. Each individual responded to our initial invitation with a resounding yes. They were each enthusiastic about being involved in what they felt would be a unique and worthwhile contribution to singing and vocal education. Their generosity has been exceptional, their expertise unquestionable and their love of singing and music education inspiring. The writings within, presented by them, are based on years of study and experience from a variety of educational and professional levels.

Profound thanks and admiration are extended to Brian Winnie, editor and coordinator of this volume. Brian could, and should, write a book on organization and management; his skills are incredible! He is a creative and talented individual to whom I owe a great deal of thanks for his tireless work on this project. Brian went about the task of selecting authors, organizing and collecting materials, motivating writers and editing text with energy and enthusiasm. He is an educator of the highest order that is apparent in the composition of this volume. Thanks to Brian Winnie, the world now has a collection of interesting and insightful articles contained in one volume written by many of today's most prominent voice teachers, choral teachers, voice researchers, and vocologists. To Shawn Girsberger my unending gratitude for her work with Meredith Music Publications and for the artistic layout and cover design of this volume. And finally, to the thousands of music students and their directors who have inspired each of us, our never-ending thanks for your dedication, beautiful music making and the belief that music does make a difference.

Garwood Whaley
*President and Founder,*
*Meredith Music Publications*

❧ ❧ ❧

My extreme gratitude goes to Gar for this opportunity and his willingness to have this topic included within the "Cookbook Series." My heartfelt thanks to each author who took time from their professional lives to contribute stellar recipes without remuneration. I am grateful for their collegiality, generosity, work ethic, and sense of humor throughout the process. May this book also connect each of you to one another in the field.

To the National Association of Teachers of Singing, thank you for your continued support of vocal education and voice science research. I hope the royalties from this project help to support those future endeavors.

Finally, I give thanks to my colleagues, family, partner, students, and friends who supported this project and my love of cooking.

Brian J. Winnie
*Project Coordinator/Editor*

## About the Authors

**Valerie Accetta**, M.F.A., is the Head of Musical Theatre at the University of Alabama at Birmingham and a Certified Master Teacher of Estill Voice Training. An Equity actress, she played Margy in the First National Tour of *State Fair*, starring John Davidson. Valerie holds a B.A. in Musical Theatre Pedagogy from Otterbein University and an M.F.A. in Theatre Pedagogy from Virginia Commonwealth University. Her directing credits include *South Pacific*, *Avenue Q*, and *Spring Awakening*.

**Diana Allan**, D.M.A., has appeared in operatic and concert performances nationally and internationally, including Mexico, Germany, Czech Republic, Italy, and Brazil. In over 26 years on the University of Texas at San Antonio faculty, her students have enjoyed success at local, regional, and national levels. Dr. Allan's website, www.musicpeakperformance.com has been visited by performers from 185 countries. She is author of *The Mindful Musicians Physical and Mental Strategies for Optimal Performance* (2018) and *The Relaxed Musician: Mental Preparation for Confident Performances* (2012).

**Shellie Beeman**, D.A., is a lyric soprano and a Certified McClosky Voice Technician, often working with ENT/SLP referred clients as they rebuild their voices. She completed her D.A. degree in Voice Performance with a Secondary Emphasis in Speech-Language Pathology from Ball State University. Shellie teaches college voice courses and applied voice lessons and is an active performer and conference clinician. She enjoys traveling and presenting on vocal health for the professional voice user.

**Geoffrey Boers**, D.M.A., is Director of Choral Activities at the University of Washington in Seattle, a program widely recognized as forward thinking, vibrant, and of great distinction. Under his direction, the graduate choral program has developed a singular mission: to nurture the whole student as conductor-teacher-servant-leader-scholar. Boers also sings professionally and is the conductor of the Symphony Tacoma Voices where he conducts both the choir and symphony in a four-concert season.

**Nancy Bos**, independent voice teacher in the Seattle area, is author of *The Teen Girl's Singing Guide: Tips for Making Singing the Center of Your Life* and *Singing 101: Vocal Basics and Fundamental Singing Skills for All Styles and Abilities*. In the "Every Sing" podcast, Nancy interviews musicians about their passion for singing. Nancy has worked in the recording industry, film, theater, with the Seattle Symphony, and toured Europe as a mezzo soloist. www.nancybos.net

**Kenneth Bozeman**, Professor at Lawrence University, holds performance degrees from Baylor University and the University of Arizona, and studied at the Conservatory of Music in Munich. He has received two Lawrence awards for excellence in teaching and the Van Lawrence Fellowship by the Voice Foundation for his interest in voice science. He is the author of *Practical Vocal Acoustics: Pedagogic Applications for Teachers and Singers* and *Kinesthetic Voice Pedagogy: Motivating Acoustic Efficiency*.

**Karen Brunssen** is on the voice faculty of the Bienen School of Music at Northwestern University where she is Co-Chair of Music Performance. Her book *The Evolving Singing Voice: Changes Across the Life Span* will be released in summer 2018. She will be installed as President of the National Association of Teachers of Singing in 2018. She has been a frequent master teacher, presenter, clinician, and adjudicator throughout the United States, Canada, Switzerland, England, and China.

**Terry Chasteen** teaches singing at Western Illinois University School of Music where he was recognized with an Excellence in Teaching Award. After completing the Estill Voice Training Courses during his most recent sabbatical project, Terry has expanded his teaching students interested in CCM and served as the voice teacher and coordinator for the Professional Training Program for Musical Theatre Interns in conjunction with Theatre West Virginia. He continues to perform professionally as a classical and theatre soloist.

**Steven R. Chicurel-Stein**, D.M.A., is Associate Director of the School of Performing Arts and Professor of Theatre at The University of Central Florida. He earned Bachelor, Master, and Doctor of Musical Arts degrees from Mars Hill University, The Peabody Conservatory of Music, and The University of Kentucky respectively. A Certified Course Instructor of Estill Voice International, Chicurel-Stein was the 2013 Estill Lifetime Achievement Award recipient. He is a published author and active voice clinician worldwide.

**Mindy Damon**, Ed.D., enjoys a stylistically diverse musical career that includes national and international vocal performances of jazz, pop, opera, worship and musical theatre styles. From Walt Disney World's "Voices of Liberty" in Orlando to Sea World in San Diego, she continues to balance singing with teaching and research with her twenty-three years of collegiate voice teaching. Dr. Damon is currently a Professor of Voice and Commercial Music at Liberty University.

**James F. Daugherty**, Ph.D., is an emeritus professor at the University of Kansas where he directed the School of Music Vocal/Choral Pedagogy Research Group and its Vocology Laboratory. He continues to lecture nationally and internationally and to publish in the major research journals related to singing and vocal music education.

**Kristin Dauphinais**, D.M.A., is an associate professor at the University of Arizona. She has also served as a member of the voice faculty at the Saarburger Serenaden Chamber Music Festival (Germany), AIMS in Graz (Austria) and the Opera festival de San Luis (Mexico). An active performer she has performed with orchestras, opera companies and in concert in the United States, Germany, Austria, Italy, Luxembourg, England, China, Australia, Spain, Brazil, Mexico and Costa Rica.

**Rollo Dilworth**, D.M.A., is Professor of Choral Music Education and Chair of Music Education and Therapy at Temple University's Boyer College of Music in Philadelphia, PA. His choral publications can be found in the catalogs of Hal Leonard, Colla Voce, and Santa Barbara. His choral pedagogy books entitled *Choir Builders* have been widely circulated among elementary, secondary, community, and church choral directors. Dilworth frequently serves as a guest conductor and/or clinician for festival and all-state choirs throughout the United States and abroad.

**Kate Duncan** is a professional vocalist and director of the Popular & Commercial Music program at Loyola University New Orleans, where she teaches applied vocal study, music theory, artist development, artist health & wellness, and directs two contemporary vocal ensembles. She earned a bachelor's degree in vocal performance and English from Westminster College (PA) and a Master of Music degree from the University of Minnesota. Her past teachers have included Kristi Dearing, Janet Kane, Tina Thielen-Gaffey, and Kim Nazarian.

**Rosana Eckert** is an internationally renowned jazz vocalist, composer, and educator. She performs throughout the U.S. and abroad, and her recordings, *At the End of the Day* and *Small Hotel*, have received critical recognition. She teaches jazz voice, song writing, and vocal pedagogy at the University of North Texas and is the author of *Singing with Expression: A Guide to Authentic & Adventurous Song Interpretation*. Rosana also works regularly as a studio vocalist and voice-over actor, having worked on hundreds of commercials and recording projects heard worldwide.

**Michael Edward Edgerton**, D.M.A., is a composer and at the forefront of vocal exploration by extending the capabilities of voice through the use of voice science and psychoacoustics. Michael's music coalesces diverse influences such as European avant-garde, American experimentalism, and world music into contexts that are influenced by science. His artistic mission is to liberate sounds that otherwise remain in danger of being overlooked. Michael has received prizes for his compositions, which are performed around the world.

**Matthew Edwards** is an associate professor and coordinator of musical theatre voice at Shenandoah Conservatory. He is also Artistic Director of the CCM Vocal Pedagogy Institute. He is the author of, *So You Want to Sing Rock 'N' Roll?* and numerous articles for *Journal of Voice*, *Journal of Singing*, *Southern Theatre*, *American Music Teacher*, *VoicePrints*, and many others. Edwards is regularly invited to teach workshops and master classes for universities, NATS chapters, and conferences throughout the world. Online at EdwardsVoice.com.

**Robert Edwin** has been a professional singer since 1965, a published ASCAP songwriter since 1967, a published author since 1968, and an independent studio singing teacher and coach since 1975. A leading authority on Contemporary Commercial Music (CCM) and child voice pedagogy, Mr. Edwin is an internationally-recognized master teacher and clinician; an Associate Editor for the NATS *Journal of Singing*, and a member of the distinguished American Academy of Teachers of Singing (AATS). www.robertedwinstudio.com

**Patrick K. Freer**, Ed.D., is Professor of Music at Georgia State University. He has conducted choirs and/or presented in nearly all USA states and dozens of countries throughout the world. He has authored books, DVDs, and over 120 articles in most of the field's leading national and international journals. His research focuses on the experience of adolescent boys during the voice change. Freer is a recent inductee of the Westminster Choir College Music Education Hall of Fame.

**J.D. Frizzell**, D.M.A., is the Director of Fine Arts at Briarcrest Christian School in Memphis, TN. He earned his Doctor of Musical Arts Degree in Choral Conducting degree from The University of Kentucky. He has dozens of best-selling compositions with major publishing houses. Dr. Frizzell is the co-founder and President of The A Cappella Education Association. His a cappella group, OneVoice, is a SONY Recording Artist. Dr. Frizzell is active as an adjudicator, clinician, and guest conductor.

**Jeannie Gagné,** M.A., is a performer, author, and songwriter hailing from NYC with an eclectic musical background including jazz, classical, and pop/rock. She's worked with artists including Philip Glass, Bare Naked Ladies, Cher, Patti Austin, and George Duke, and appeared on television, radio, movie soundtracks, recordings, and international tours. Voice Professor at Berklee College of Music, Ms. Gagné is expert in vocal pedagogy, including healthy technique for contemporary genres. Her popular YouTube series "The Vocal Genie" reaches viewers around the world.

**Kelly K. Garner**, D.M.A., is an Assistant Professor of Commercial Voice at Belmont University. She has received Dove and BMI Award nominations for Song of the Year and Most Performed Gospel Song, and she performed as a backing vocalist with numerous artists including Gloria Estefan. She is the founder of Big Dog Recording Studios, Yellow Tree Music Publishing Group, and Kelly Garner Productions, LLC. She has vocal coached well-established touring artists as well as *American Idol* and *The Voice* finalists. Dr. Garner completed her D.M.A. in Jazz Performance with a cognate in Music Technology from the University of Miami. She was the author of *So You Want To Sing Country*, and primary arranger for the Urban-Gospel Choral Book, *Yes & Amen!*

**Kathryn Green**, D.M.A., is a professor of voice at Shenandoah Conservatory. She received her D.M.A. in Performance at Cincinnati Conservatory of Music. She has been published in the *Journal of Voice* and in the *Journal of Singing*. Her performing career has spanned the eastern United States as well as Germany, Austria, France, and Italy. She is the executive director of the CCM Vocal Pedagogy Institute and the director of Shenandoah Conservatory's graduate vocal pedagogy program.

**Erin Hackel**, D.M.A., is an Assistant Professor at the University of Colorado, Denver. Her research and publication arc have centered on historical female belters such as Dame Vera Lynn, Yvette Guilbert, and Bokken Lasson. Erin is passionate about demystifying belt voice technique and teaching singers to sing functionally in all styles. She directs the award winning a cappella groups MIX and Lark; both groups are BOSS and SoJAM champions, winners of multiple CARA awards, and featured artists around the United States. Erin has presented workshops on healthy singing techniques, collaborative arranging, and contemporary choral techniques around the country and in Europe.

**David Harris**, D.M.A., specializes in new music, American music, and the intricacies of communication in choral singing and conducting. Living in Los Angeles, David teaches voice at the American Musical and Dramatic Academy, directs the professional choir at First Congregational Church, and is the co-founder and director of VoiceScienceWorks. David has a D.M.A. in choral conducting from the University of Colorado and attended the Summer Vocology Institute with Dr. Ingo Titze.

**Matthew Hoch**, D.M.A., is Associate Professor of Voice and Coordinator of Voice Studies at Auburn University, as well as Choirmaster and Minister of Music at Holy Trinity Episcopal Church in Auburn, Alabama. He holds a B.M. from Ithaca College with a triple major in vocal performance, music education, and music theory; an M.M. from the Hartt School with a double major in vocal performance and music history; and a D.M.A. from the New England Conservatory in vocal performance.

**Laurel Irene** is a vocal artist and voice educator based in Los Angeles and the co-founder of VoiceScienceWorks. As a performer, she explores vocal repertoire ranging from Monteverdi to Mozart to the wacky, wild, and extreme sounds of the 21st century. A graduate of the Summer Vocology Institute, she gives workshops across the country and presentations at conferences including the Pan-American Vocology Association, the American Choral Directors Association, and the Acoustical Society of America.

**Craig Hella Johnson** is the Artistic Director of Conspirare, Cincinnati Vocal Arts Ensemble Music Director and Victoria Bach Festival's Conductor Emeritus. Johnson is Artist in Residence, Professor of Practice at Texas State University. Johnson and Conspirare were recognized with a 2014 Grammy® for Best Choral Performance. Chorus America honored Johnson with the Michael Korn Founders Award for Development of the Professional Choral Art and the Texas State Legislature named him Texas State Musician for 2013.

**LaToya Lain**, D.M.A., a native of New Orleans, Louisiana, has been applauded for her "wonderfully rich" and "powerful" voice. She studied voice at the University of Cincinnati-College Conservatory of Music, Florida State University, and the University of Nevada. Dr. Lain's recent engagements include a performance as the soprano soloist in Ralph Vaughan Williams' *Dona Nobis Pacem* in Stern Auditorium at Carnegie Hall, and solo recitals at the American Church in Paris and the Dutch Reform Church in Harare, Zimbabwe. She continues to present recitals, masterclasses, and workshops at numerous American colleges and universities. Dr. Lain currently serves on the voice faculty of Central Michigan University.

**Rachel Lebon**, Ph.D., is Professor at Frost School of Music at the University of Miami and served on faculty at Belmont College. She has toured with "Tops in Blue" of the U.S. Air Force and has toured the Soviet Union and Portugal. Dr. Lebon has been a professional vocalist and studio singer in Dallas/Ft. Worth, Nashville, and Miami. She is the author of *The Professional Vocalist* and *The Versatile Vocalist* and has published articles in *Journal of Voice*.

**Heather Lyle**, M.M., is a National Center for Voice and Speech Vocologist, a certified teacher of Fitzmaurice Voicework® and a certified yoga teacher. She operates a private studio in LA and has taught at USC, Santa Monica College, LA Mission College, The Hong Kong Academy of Performing Arts and Loreto College, India. Heather is the creator of The Heather Lyle Vocal Yoga Method® that uses yoga therapy and primal voice use to free the voice.

**Valerie Lippoldt Mack**, Chair of Music and Dance at Butler Community College in El Dorado, KS is recognized as a music educator and professional choreographer throughout the United States. Her choreography has been featured at Carnegie Hall, Disney World, national music conventions, Miss America and various national show choir competitions and festivals around the country. Valerie's best-selling *Ice Breaker* books are published with Shawnee Press as well as her newest resource book, *Putting the SHOW in CHOIR*.

**Brian Manternach**, D.MUS., is Assistant Professor in the University of Utah's Department of Theatre. He has given presentations for the Voice Foundation, PAVA, the National Center for Voice and Speech, TEDxSaltLakeCity, and for NATS at chapter, regional, and national conferences. He is a past recipient of the NATS Foundation Voice Pedagogy Award, is an Associate Editor of the *Journal of Singing*, and authors "The Singer's Library" column for *Classical Singer*. Learn more at www.brianmanternach.com.

**Lori McCann**, D.M.A., is Associate Professor and Coordinator of Vocal Performance at the John J. Cali School of Music, Montclair State University. She is the current Eastern Region Governor, for the National Association of Teachers of Singing (NATS) and in the summers, she serves as Artist Faculty for the American Institute of Musical Studies (AIMS) in Graz, Austria. As a soprano soloist, Lori McCann has performed extensively in opera and concert in Europe and the U.S. and has won many competitions and awards including National Finalist in the Metropolitan Opera National Council Auditions.

**Samantha Miller**, D.M.A., is an Associate Professor of Voice at Liberty University where she specializes in hybrid training for the versatile performer. Dr. Miller is an active and seasoned classical and commercial performer, having just released her first album with All Peoples Church called *The Sound of Revival*. Her research on Stephen Collins Foster has been published in *Music in American Life: An Encyclopedia of the Songs, Styles, Stars, and Stories that Shaped Our Culture*.

**Jeremy Ryan Mossman**, M.M., is a Music Theatre voice specialist and repertoire coach who has taught in a variety of universities and colleges in Ontario, Michigan, and is currently on the music faculty at Carthage College in Kenosha, WI. His pedagogy is holistic as a Certified Master Teacher of Estill Voice Training, a certified yoga teacher, and currently in a training program to become a *Guild Certified Feldenkrais Practitioner®*.

**Dawn Wells Neely**, D.M.A., is Assistant Professor of Voice and Director of Opera Workshop at the University of West Georgia. Dr. Neely received her Doctor of Musical Arts from the University of Alabama. She sings and directs opera, oratorio, and chamber ensembles. Dr. Neely's research interests include body awareness and alignment methods for musicians. Dr. Neely earned her 200 Level Yoga Teaching Certificate through the Yoga Alliance in 2014.

**Corinne Ness**, Ph.D., is dean and associate professor of voice at Carthage College. Equally at home teaching classical and contemporary music, her students have gone on to professional careers in performance, directing, and teaching. She has presented at conferences across the United States, focusing on voice technique and style. Dr. Ness is the creator and director of a Visiting Scholars program for Chinese teachers and travels frequently to Shanghai and Beijing as a guest professor.

**Kate Paradise** is a jazz and popular music educator, vocal musician, ensemble director and arranger specializing in singing, voice science, and improvisation. She currently serves as the Assistant Director of the School of Music at Belmont University. Kate holds a B.M. and M.M. from the University of Miami and certifications in both Vocology and Somatic Voicework™. While teaching and performing in Nashville, TN, Kate is also pursuing a D.M.A. at the University of Illinois, Champaign-Urbana.

**Lisa Popeil**, M.F.A., in Voice, is the creator of the Voiceworks® Method and is based in Los Angeles. She offers the *Total Singer DVD*, Total Singer Workshop, and the book *Sing Anything- Mastering Vocal Styles*. A frequent presenter at international voice conferences, Lisa specializes in commercial voice technique and the pedagogy of belting. Lisa has also contributed to *Oxford Handbook of Singing*, *Oxford Handbook of Music Education*, *Journal of Voice*, and *Journal of Singing*.

**Kathy Kessler Price**, Ph.D., teaches voice and voice science/pedagogy courses at Westminster Choir College where she is an Associate Professor of Voice and directs both the Presser Voice Lab and the Voice Pedagogy Institute. As a soprano soloist, she has performed at such distinguished venues as The Kennedy Center, National Museum for Women in the Arts, and The White House. She is the co-author of *The Anatomy of Tone*, a voice science-based choral pedagogy book.

**Kate Reid**, D.M.A., is an associate professor and director of Jazz Vocal Performance in the Studio Music and Jazz department at the Frost School of Music. A member of SAG/AFTRA, Kate has lent her voice to many film soundtracks, television and commercial spots. A jazz vocalist and pianist, Kate performs in jazz venues in Los Angeles and Miami. She is in demand as a guest artist, clinician and conductor throughout the U.S. and Canada.

**Kat Reinhert**, Ph.D., is an experienced vocalist, songwriter and educator and has released four independent albums of original music and covers. She holds a B.M. in Jazz/ Commercial Voice from The Manhattan School of Music, an M.M. in Jazz Performance/Pedagogy and a Ph.D. in Music Education, both from the University of Miami. Kat is the Vice President for the Association for Popular Music Education and the Head of Contemporary Voice at The University of Miami, FL.

**Trineice Robinson-Martin**, Ed.D, is an award winning pedagogue, international performer, and scholar. She specializes in vocal pedagogy and teaching strategies for singing African American music styles. She is the creator of Soul Ingredients™ Methodology; jazz voice instructor and ensemble director at Princeton University; Executive Director of African American Jazz Caucus, Inc.; national faculty for the Gospel Music Workshop of America, Incorporated; Creative Arts director at Turning Point United Methodist Church; and maintains a private voice studio in NJ.

**Marci Rosenberg**, M.S. CCC, is a Speech Pathologist/Voice & Singing Specialist at the University of Michigan Vocal Health Center specializing in rehabilitation of injured voices. She is featured guest faculty at the new CCM Vocal Pedagogy Institute at Shenandoah and is co-author of *The Vocal Athlete* and *The Vocal Athlete: Application and technique for the hybrid singer*. Currently, she is serving as Vice President for the Pan American Vocology Association (PAVA). Marci maintains a private voice studio in Ann Arbor, MI.

**Katharin Rundus**, D.M.A., is a voice teacher, a singer and a choral conductor. She is the Director of Vocal Studies at Fullerton College, where in addition to teaching private voice and voice classes, she has conducted the Fullerton College Chamber Singers and the Women's Chorale. She also maintains a voice studio at the Bob Cole Conservatory of Music of the California State University at Long Beach. She is the author of three books on vocal and choral pedagogy; *Cantabile*, *Cantabile Voice Class*, and *Choral Cantabile* all from Pavane Publishing.

**Deke Sharon** (Vocal Arrangements). Heralded as "The Father of Contemporary A Cappella," (Entertainment Weekly), Deke is responsible for the current sound of modern a cappella. Deke produced "The Sing-Off" worldwide and served as arranger, on-site music director, and vocal producer for Universal's "Pitch Perfect 1, 2 & 3." Deke founded the Contemporary A Cappella Society and is also contemporary a cappella's most prolific arranger, having arranged over 2,000 songs. His published books include *Acappella Arranging*, *A Cappella*, *The Heart of Vocal Harmony*, *A Cappella Warmups for Pop and Jazz Choir*, and *So You Want to Sing A Cappella.*

**Stephen Sieck**, D.M.A., serves as Co-Director of Choral Studies and Chair of the Voice Department at the Lawrence University Conservatory of Music in Appleton, WI. A graduate of the University of Chicago and University of Illinois at Urbana-Champaign, Steve directs choirs and teaches conducting and choral rehearsal techniques at Lawrence. His book *Teaching with Respect: Inclusive Pedagogy for Choral Directors* is published by Hal Leonard and discusses in detail the challenges and strategies of teaching all students well.

**Loraine Sims**, D.M.A., Associate Professor, Edith Killgore Kirkpatrick Professor of Voice at Louisiana State University. Presentations include "*Training Transgender Singers for Opera Performance: Gender Bending Beyond the Pants Role*" for the 2017 NOA Conference, "*Teaching Lucas: A Transgender Student's Vocal Journey from Soprano to Tenor*" at the 2017 ICVT, the 2016 National NOA/NATS conference, the 2016 National MTNA Conference, and the 2016 National NATS Convention, and "*Training the Terrible Tongue!*" for the 2012 National NATS Conference.

**Linda J. Snyder** is Professor Emerita of Voice and Opera at the University of Dayton. Previously she taught voice, opera, and musical theatre at New York University, Illinois Wesleyan University, Midland Lutheran College, and the National Music Camp at Interlochen. An active soprano, collaborative pianist, author, adjudicator, conductor and visiting clinician on the national and international levels, Dr. Snyder currently serves as President of the National Association of Teachers of Singing (2016-2018).

**Kimberly Steinhauer**, Ph.D., devoted her career to voice earning a B.S. in Music Education from Indiana University of Pennsylvania, M.A. in Speech Communication from The Pennsylvania State University, and Ph.D. in Communication Science and Disorders from the University of Pittsburgh. She has presented internationally and is published in the *Journal of Voice*, *Emotions in the Human Voice*, and *Professional Voice: The Science and Art of Clinical Care*. She is President and Founding Partner of Estill Voice International, LLC.

**Peter Thoresen**, D.M., is an award-winning voice teacher, countertenor and music director. His students appear regularly on and off Broadway, in national tours, on TV and film, and record for the Columbia and Broadway Record labels. Thoresen works internationally with students as a voice teacher, music director and collaborator in Pakistan, Turkmenistan and Indonesia as a faculty member of American Voices and is a voice professor at Pace University. He performs throughout the US and abroad.

**Cynthia Vaughn** is the Associate Editor for "Independent Voices" for National Association of Teachers of Singing (NATS) *InterNos*; founder of NATS Chats online discussions; and former Vocal Literature Coordinator for NATS Intern Program. Cynthia Vaughn and Meribeth Dayme co-authored the leading voice class textbook and song anthology, *The Singing Book*, now in its 3rd edition with W.W. Norton publishers. Vaughn is a former editor and feature writer for *Classical Singer* magazine.

**Catherine A. Walker**, Associate Professor of Musical Theatre, University of Michigan, is a music director, conductor, vocal coach, and accompanist. Ms. Walker has been recognized by the University of Michigan for her outstanding contributions as a classroom instructor as well as curriculum development. In addition, Ms. Walker is an Estill trained Certified Master Teacher and remains active as a clinician, vocal coach, choral conductor and theatrical music director.

**Edrie Means Weekly**, is Co-Founder of the CCM Vocal Pedagogy Institute, and was a NATS Intern Program Master Teacher in 2013. Her students are featured on Grammy Recordings, Movies, Broadway, National/International Tours and TV. She has published articles in the Journal of Voice and a sub-chapter in Teaching Singing in the 21st Century. She regularly presents CCM research, workshops and masterclasses at the Voice Foundation, NATS, PAVA, STEC's national conferences and universities throughout the United States. Edrie is recorded by Decca and Koch. http://edriemeans.wix.com/edriemeans

**Brian J. Winnie**, D.M.A., is the Director of Choral Activities & Voice and Chair of the Music Department at Southwestern College (Kansas). He has worked with festival choirs throughout the United States and in Russia; has presented workshops at NAfME and ACDA conferences, and at the Estill World Voice Symposium; and is a Certified Master Teacher and Certified Course Instructor-Candidate in Estill Voice Training. Dr. Winnie has published articles in *Voice and Speech Review* and *ChorTeach*.

**Alan Zabriskie**, Ph.D., is Director of Choral Studies at Texas Tech University where he serves as conductor of the University Choir and teaches choral conducting. He holds the Ph.D. from The Florida State University. Alan's choirs have performed at a National Convention of ACDA and as the headline choir for the Missouri Music Educators Association In-service Workshop/Conference. Alan's textbook, *Foundations of Choral Tone*, has been adopted by numerous universities and choral conductors around the world.

RECIPE

# Get the Best Ingredients: A Recipe for Recruiting

*Valerie Accetta*

Strong, talented students are the best way to promote a voice studio or program. With so many programs and teachers, identifying and attracting these students can be challenging. Teachers can make the search easier by utilizing social media, current students, and chocolate chip cookies.

**INGREDIENTS:**
Tickets to a local performance
A free workshop
Social media savvy
A friendly student
Personalized visits
Homemade chocolate chip cookies

**SERVES:**
The growth of a studio or program; future recruiting efforts.

The first step is to identify potential students. Locally, attend a high school, community choral, or theatre performance. Get to know the director or teacher of the group, and personally congratulate talented students on their strong performances. To reach a national audience, attend large gatherings of students at competitions like:

- The National Association of Teachers of Singing, (www.nats.org)
- The Southeastern Theatre Conference (www.setc.org)
- The International Thespians Conference (www.schooltheatre.org/international-thespiansociety/home)

Once you have identified the students, you now need to let them know about you. The best way to do this is to work with them. Offer a free workshop at a local high school or at a conference. Promote your studio by giving a day of free lessons to students from a particular school. This personal interaction helps to develop a relationship with potential students and gives them a sense of your teaching style.

Get the word out about your services on social media. Tweet about any upcoming performances of your students. Post photos of lessons or rehearsals on Instagram. Congratulate a local high school group on their stellar performance on Facebook. Target specific schools and students that would be a good match for your studio or program and send them personalized email reminders about upcoming performances or auditions.

Now, you need to get your current students involved. Potential students identify more strongly to their peers, so asking your friendliest student to reach out to a potential recruit can go a long way. Additionally, let all of your students know how important it is that they represent your studio or program well. Their performances and behavior reflect on your program, and when your students are warm and welcoming, potential recruits and their parents will spread the word on social media and blogs such as College Confidential (www.collegeconfidential.com).

Once the word is out and potential students start contacting you, it is important to arrange a personalized visit of your studio or program. For the private voice teacher, this is easy to do by scheduling a discussion to answer any questions and to share the expectations of your studio. This proves more difficult for a larger institution, which may have several visitors each semester. In this case, every visit should be arranged with care. Pair each visitor with a current student. Set up an itinerary where they will be able to attend classes, watch a rehearsal or performance, and meet with members of the faculty. With larger institutions, these visits can mean the difference between gaining one of these students or losing them to another program, and again, word gets out on social media.

Finally, give them cookies. While this may sound trivial, it has honestly been a cornerstone of the recruiting efforts at the University of Alabama at Birmingham. Whether auditioning students on campus or at a unified audition in another city, my colleague, Carolyn Violi (a phenomenal baker) gives every auditioning student a homemade cookie to get them through the long day. In later correspondence with these students, many of them mention the cookie and comment on how special it was to them. The cookies are not our way of "standing out from the crowd." Carolyn wants each student to feel valued and cared for. Whether or not these students get into your program or end up studying with you, they remember that you treated them as a unique individual and they tell their friends.

Every interaction with a potential student is important. Even in programs or studios that see hundreds of auditioning recruits each year, acknowledging the worth and humanity of each student will continue to attract the best and the brightest. Promoting your training opportunities with honest and kind interactions will yield tremendous growth for your studio or program.

RECIPE

# Tips and Tricks for Scrumptious, Confident Performances

*Diana Allan*

Performers, like chefs, often deal with varying levels of performance anxiety over whether an audience or critic will enjoy their performance, or "dish." In a survey entitled, "Mental Skills Necessary for Performing at Peak Levels" (Allan & Cohn, 2010) over 500 musicians identified five primary challenges that performers face: 1.) worrying or caring too much what others think, 2.) lacking confidence, 3.) lacking trust in learned skills, 4.) needing to be perfect, and 5.) fear or performance anxiety. In order to play or sing at peak levels, performers who are motivated to do so, can learn to believe strongly in themselves and their abilities, can learn the difference between effective practice and performance skills, and can learn to focus on what is most important and shift back quickly when distracted.

**INGREDIENTS:**

Strong motivation to grow and learn
A strong belief in self and ability
An effective practice and performance mindset
A sharp focus on *controllables* in performance
The ability to shift focus quickly when it strays
Declaring practice complete
Simulating performance

**SERVES:**

Anyone who experiences performance anxiety that adversely affects performance and anyone who desires to play or sing exuberant, exciting, confident, ________________ (insert your own descriptive adjective), and fun performances.

**PREP:**

1. **A Dash of Anxiety.** It is no wonder that performers often get nervous, feel butterflies in their stomachs, or experience anxiety. Performing, whether as a teacher in front of a classroom, a conductor on the podium, or as a musician on the stage, is a demanding, heightened experience—one that we have actually chosen. The problem with music performance anxiety, like food when you are dieting, is that each individual needs a moderate amount of *arousal* or *activation* in order to deliver a peak performance. Contrary to what you might have previously thought, this means that we don't want to eliminate anxiety, as that could result in flat, uninteresting performances, but learn to harness and manage the energy we need.

2. **Embrace Mistakes.** There are many strategies performers can use to perform their best under pressure. The first is to possess a strong *motivation* to grow and learn. Conversely, many performers have a strong motivation to prove they are good enough. This leads to disappointment, fear, and anxiety. Instead, when you are motivated to grow and learn, you embrace mistakes and challenges as lessons to help you improve. This attitude helps you view feedback and critique as information you can use to improve your performance, not as a referendum on your talent and ability.
3. **Add Confidence.** Once you are effectively motivated, you need to have a strong belief in yourself and your abilities—*confidence*. Confidence is not something we are born with. It is a belief system that must be nurtured. One way to do this is to construct a *Confidence Resume*. This is a list of reasons why you should believe strongly in yourself such as, *I am very dedicated*, or *I won that important audition last year*. Many of us need reminding of the good things about our performing. (Heaven knows, we don't need reminding of all the challenging things!)
4. **Simulate Performance.** A strong belief in yourself and your abilities can be fostered or inhibited by the way you practice. All performers need two skillsets—a *practice mindset* and a *performance mindset*. Practice skills are specific skills that are necessary to improve and refine technical ability. It is easy to get stuck in this mindset because we practice much more than we perform. That is why it is so important to cultivate the performance mindset—skills like acceptance and trust—in order to maintain a clear and present focus and trust ourselves and our preparation. Simulating performance in every practice and declaring practice complete one or two days prior to performances are effective strategies to shift into the performance mindset.
5. **Focus in the Present.** Simulating performance is also an ideal way to practice the kind of *focus* necessary for effective performing. Many performers become distracted by a focus on things that are outside of their control—mistakes they have just made, the audience, or other performers. Confident performers focus first on their preparation, both musical and mental, interacting and responding to the music, and when distracted are quick to shift their focus back to the present moment.

So, whether you perform in the kitchen, in the classroom, on the podium, or on the stage, you, too, can learn to give scrumptious, confident performances.

RECIPE

# A Recipe for Relaxation and Fighting Vocal Fatigue

*Shellie Beeman*

A thriving, reliable voice is key to the success of any voice teacher wishing to perform, teach, or juggle both. Many teachers experience symptoms of vocal fatigue, calling it "normal wear and tear" of a busy and stressful schedule. Finding freedom and energy for your voice allows you to communicate freely with students and colleagues, and enjoy a successful singing and teaching career.

**INGREDIENTS:**
Soft, relaxed hands
A few, quiet moments
A mirror
An engaged and relaxed mind and body
A heightened sense of kinesthetic awareness
Daily consistency (2–5 times per day is recommended)
Perform for 5–15 minutes per repetition

**SERVES:**
The singing, speaking, and "teaching" voice.
The healthy or dysfunctional voice.

Vocal fatigue is often described as "tired voice;" an ache or tightness in the throat or voice at the end of a teaching session, day, or week; effortful speaking or singing; loss of pitches; hoarseness at the end of the day or week; etc. Contributing factors include muscular tension from stress, poor alignment, and improper breathing; incorrect speaking pitch, range, and volumes; insufficient resonance; harsh and unsupported glottals and fry; overuse; tension in the articulators, neck, or throat. You can often have control over what causes this fatigue by applying the following recipe and exercises to relax muscles when using your voice.

1. **Posture** is the support structure for respiration and phonation. Balancing your weight equally, stand with your feet shoulder width apart and knees unlocked. Allow the spine to lengthen from bottom to top, feeling the lower lumbar area release under you with a slight pelvic tilt. With this spinal alignment, you should feel the rib cage and chest cavity open and lift. The shoulders are neither hunched nor thrust back. The neck should feel like an extension of the spine, with the head balancing on top of the A–O joint at the base of the skull.

2. **Breath** is the power source for phonation. With this aligned and buoyant posture, allow the inhalation to come to you. Do not reach for it. Allow it to drop into the body, expanding low in the abdominal area and base of the rib cage. As you exhale, the rib cage should remain open while the abdominal muscles gently and slowly contract inward. Remember: Breathe; Breathe low; Breathe often!
3. **Six Areas of Relaxation**:
   The following exercises are cumulative. Maintain Steps 1 and 2, posture and breath, while performing them.
   - **Face**: Using the pads of the fingers, slowly massage the muscles of the face with small, circular movements. Start at the hairline and move down and around the face, covering the forehead, eyebrows, temples, cheeks, sides of the nose, jaw muscles, lips, and chin. Your face should fall with relaxation.
   - **Tongue**: Let your tongue soften and relax inside your mouth. Allow your mouth to open as the tongue releases forward. Only stretch the tongue out of the mouth as far as it will remain rounded. Avoid spreading the lips or tensing the jaw. Slowly allow the tongue to return inside the mouth. Repeat.
   - **Swallowing Muscles**: The action of the swallowing muscles may be felt under the chin. Similar to kneading dough, massage these muscles starting in the center and inside the line of the jawbone with the pads of your thumbs. Use an up-and-down motion rather than side-to-side, avoiding the larynx. These muscles should feel soft.
   - **Jaw**: Take your chin in your hand with your thumb under and forefinger on top. Slowly and freely move the jaw up and down by relaxing the muscles at the hinge of the jaw.
   - **Larynx**: Locate the thyroid cartilage of the larynx (Adam's apple) and hold lightly on either side between the thumb and forefinger of one hand. Move your larynx gently and slowly from side to side, imitating a subtle wiggle.
   - **Neck**: Let your head fall forward, chin to chest, allowing the weight of the head to stretch the neck muscles gently. Slowly raise your head back up, and lazily draw a small figure eight or imitate a tiny "yes/no" nod. Your head should feel light and balanced at the top of the spine/A–O joint.[1]
4. **Breathy Sigh and "Hum-Mum-Mums"**: After checking posture, breathing, and the six areas, breathe comfortably for 2–3 repetitions with your mouth open. With the [a] vowel in mind, inhale again, and upon the release of the breath for exhalation, emit a downward, light, audible sigh in a comfortable pitch range on the [a] vowel. Keep the breath engaged to the end, allowing for a steady stream of air to create flow phonation. One can also include [m] and "hum-mum-mum" to create ease of onset and forward resonance.

Whether you desire a healthy start or finish to the day, or you are experiencing vocal fatigue in the moment, these simple exercises are an effective, *natural* approach to resetting and reminding your vocal folds to oscillate healthfully with proper breath, relaxation, and resonance. Performing multiple resonance checks through the [m] exercises per day will help you unload the mechanism and allow for healthy, vibrant speaking and singing.

---

1 These exercises were developed by David Blair McClosky. To learn more about the McClosky Technique, please see David Blair McClosky, *Your Voice at its Best: Enhancement for the Healthy Voice, Help for the Troubled Voice* (Long Grove, IL: Waveland Press, 2011). The McClosky Institute of Voice at https://www.mcclosky.org, and Maria Argyros, "An Introduction to the McClosky Technique," *Vocapedia*, 2015, http://www.vocapedia.info/cgi/page.cgi/5/_articles.html/Pedagogy/An_Introduction_to_the_McClosky_Technique.

RECIPE

# No Utensils Allowed: Using Your Hands to Discover Appoggio

*Geoffrey Boers*

Through the study of mirror neurons, scientists are researching the part of the brain that fires when we do an action or observe someone else doing an action. The possibility that a person can learn by observing and by kinesthetic activity has profound implications in teaching voice. By pairing specific gestures with specific sensations of singing, gestures become a metaphor of the singing mechanism, be it functions of resonance or *appoggio*. When utilizing the gestures, a student can achieve a greater sense of body awareness, and remember and re-awaken the paired sensations and functions as they develop new techniques. *Appoggio*, or to lean, refers to the balanced effort of numerous muscle groups working independently, each "leaning" in unique manners to create a relaxed and natural sensation during phonation. This recipe is developed to help singers access the parts of the body engaged in creating *appoggio*.

**INGREDIENTS:**
1 "Triangle of the Voice" Set-up
1 "Scissors" Gesture for the Glottis
1 "Round Ribs" Gesture for the Intercostals
1 "Hook-up" Gesture for the Rectus Abdominus
1 "Trap Door" Gesture for the Transverse Abdominus and Obliques

**SERVES:**
Individual singers in studio.
Group vocal technique building for choirs.
The teacher.

Each of the four balanced efforts in this recipe are paired with a corresponding gesture and activity to evoke a physical response. Each facet of *appoggio* can be taught separately and then invited to work together. These gestures, activities, and efforts place an emphasis on the *experience* of *appoggio*; first becoming familiar with the specific sensation and then able to repeat the effort. Before beginning, remember the sensation of *appoggio* is one of active ease and quiet in the body, with sensations of healthy muscle action.

**Prepare Your Ingredients:**
For each step of the recipe that follows:

1. Tell the student what part of *appoggio* they will be exploring. Show them the gesture and ask them to mirror you, or "conduct" with you.

2. Demonstrate the principle while both you and the student conduct *your* voice.
3. Draw attention to and describe the desired sensation, what it feels like to you and *without describing technically* what is happening. It is of prime importance the student works to remember the sensation *in the body* rather than try to understand and memorize the technique.
4. Invite the student to sing and conduct *with* you, then again *without* you singing. While the student sings along, you should continue to conduct with them; feeling the sensation and conducting *as if you are still singing!* You are *mirroring* for the student non-verbally.
5. If both teacher and student are focused on the *experience*, rather than trying to *understand what is happening*, the teacher can more easily *feel and sense* what the student needs to do to be more successful during the next repetition.
6. Before repeating the attempted technique, manipulate the gesture to reflect how the singer must adjust their effort.
7. Repeat step 4 with the adjusted gesture.

**Assemble:**

**The Triangle of the Voice Set-up:** To help singers "see" their instrument, put hands out in front of you as if praying in *Namaste* position. Separate hands to where the finger tips are one-inch apart, thumbs overlap, and right hand slightly above the left, creating a "broken" triangle. Begin each exercise from this starting position.

Note: We start with the triangle set-up and utilize gestures that resemble the body actions associated with singing; i.e., the expansion of the ribcage and the opening and closing of the glottis.

1. **"The Scissors" Gesture for the Glottis (opening between the vocal folds)**: From the broken triangle, with both hands, make a gesture of scissors, as in the game *Rock, Paper, Scissors*.
   a. With scissors open, and glottis open, exhale all air with no tone.
   b. Inhale, begin to exhale and close the scissors; closing the glottis so no air can pass.
   c. Practice opening the glottis suddenly as you open your fingers.
   d. Practice opening the glottis slowly, encouraging a scrape or fry sound, while gently separating your fingers.
   e. Practice closing the glottis slowly with scissors open and then close fingers to almost shut for onset.
   f. Repeat steps d. and e. with pitch.
   g. Practice varied onsets of open before sound, nearly closed, and efficient balance using a song beginning on an [a] or [o] such as *Oh, Danny Boy*.

2. **"The Round Ribs" Gesture for the Intercostals:** From the triangle, place hands on the sides of the ribcage (some may have more success feeling around the back), allow fingers to feel space between the ribs
   a. Exhale most of your air.
   b. Begin to inhale and suddenly close the glottis so no air can pass. Continue attempting to inhale.
   c. Draw attention to the sternum and upper intercostals remaining expanded, yet quiet; lower ribs expand trying to draw air in.

d. Release the glottis, as air rushes in draw attention to the expanding base of the ribs.
e. Move hands slowly back to the triangle position, keep the hands as if they were still on the ribs. Ask the student to imagine their fingers at their ribs. Repeat steps b. and c. with hands showing effort to expand the ribcage via the intercostals.
f. While demonstrating the expanding rib gesture, speak dramatically "Round ribs!" then sing those words on a single, comfortable pitch while feeling the expansion.
g. Turn hands over, as if expanding the ribcage out *from the inside,* move your hands in an arc away from your body, like a reverse breaststroke. Speak and sing with attention on the expanding gesture.

3. **The "Hook-up" Gesture for the Rectus Abdominis (RA)**: From the triangle, make a gesture that looks like the Hawaiian "hang loose," or the Texas "Hook 'em Horns" sign. Place thumbs on epigastrium at the base of the sternum with pinky fingers resting below the belly button. Cough or giggle, and feel a slight bounce or "hook."

   a. Exhale most of your air
   b. Keep left hand in place and with your right hand make an open *scissors*. Begin to inhale and close the glottis (closing fingers) so no air can pass. Continue to attempt to inhale. Feel the muscle in the place of the "hook."
   c. Draw attention to the outward movement of the epigastrium (like the "round ribs") and the tucking in and up of the pinky area.
   d. Release the glottis, as air rushes in feel the place of the "hook" droop down and out while epigastrium should remain firmly flexible moving outward.
   e. At the end of the inhalation, close the glottis again, allow the body to *relax* as the air wants to leave the body. Feel the tuck of the pinky portion of the RA, while the rest of the abdominal muscles are relaxed and intercostals expanded.
   f. Using the scissor gesture, release the glottis slowly, and exhale. Keep the body active to create a slow and steady *release* of air rather than any kind of push. Repeat with a pitch, and then a song such as *Oh, Danny Boy*.
   g. Slowly move hands out in front of you approximately six inches, ask the student to imagine that their hands are the set of muscles they were just feeling. Inhale (pinky drops with lower abs), at the end of the inhalation, cough lightly, giggling, or articulate "k," "f," "v," "z," "ng." Allow the pinky and thumb to react with the body. Ask the singer to show you what their body is doing.
   h. Repeat with gesture and pitch.

4. **The "Trap Door" Gesture for Transverse Abdominus (TrA) and Obliques (O)**: From the triangle, put hands to the sides of the belly and bend side to side; drawing attention to the softer more movable muscles.

   a. Exhale most of your air.
   b. With hands in place, begin to inhale and close the glottis so no air can pass. Continue to inhale, feel the transverse muscles attempt to pull air in by expanding sideways and down.
   c. Open the glottis, allow air to rush in, draw attention to the expanding muscles of the belly.

d. At the end of the inhalation, close the glottis again, allow the body to relax as the air wants to leave the body. Try to engage the pinky portion of the RA alone while allowing the TrA and O muscles to become soft and flexible, yet still expanded.
e. Using the scissor gesture, release the glottis slowly, and exhale. Keep the body active to create a slow and steady *release* of air rather than any kind of push. Repeat with a pitch, and then a song such as *Oh, Danny Boy*.
f. Slowly move hands out in front of you approximately six inches and directly in front of the obliques. With hands in a gesture of "curved blades," ask the student to imagine that their hands are the set of muscles they were just feeling. Inhale (the hands, as a trap door, drop with lower abdominals), at the end of the breath, cough lightly, giggling, or articulate "k," "f," "v," "z," "ng." These "dropped blades" should remain flexible during various articulations, activating only the "hook-up" gesture.
g. Repeat with gesture and pitch, and then with a song.
h. Allow these muscles to stay relatively quiet during phonation, slowly guiding the exhalation as a release without exerting tension or effort.

For videos of these exercises visit: www.geoffreyboers.com/no-utensils-allowed-supplementary-materials/

RECIPE

# Microphone Technique: Cooking Up Complex Vocals

*Nancy Bos*

Nothing lets a vocal chef whip up an outstanding interpretation better than knowing how to work their mic. Expertly mixing textures and flavors from a well-stocked pantry of vocal ingredients is best achieved through experimentation. Prepare for a world-class performance by practicing with a mic in lessons and rehearsals.

**INGREDIENTS:**
1 Dynamic Mic
1 Monitor
1 Singer

**SERVES:**
Juicy, expressive vocals from the singer to an audience who is excited to experience every nuance of the singer's interpretation.

1. Prepare the singer by showing them how the mic plugs into the monitor, how to adjust the volume, and any other features the monitor might have. Teach the singer how to create and avoid feedback by carefully moving the mic in front of the monitor, with one hand on the volume control to turn down the feedback if necessary.
2. Place the mic in the singer's light grip. Help the singer find a position for the mic at a 45-degree angle, two inches from, and slightly below, his or her bottom lip. Ask the singer to hold the mic in this position and sing one long, continuous note, breathing when needed, to create a consistent sound. While singing, instruct the singer to slowly move the mic closer and further from the mouth while listening to the sound coming from the monitor. The singer will hear variations in tone (from rich to thin) and loudness based on the mic's distance from the lips. Next, ask the singer to move the mic left and right away from the mouth to determine the range of motion for that particular mic, every mic is a little different.
3. Ask the singer to sing the word "pop" repeatedly while changing the angle and location of the mic in relationship to the lips. The "pop" sound will be less explosive if the breath passes above the mic rather than into it. However, the mic needs to receive optimal sound waves to produce the richest timbre. Holding the mic vertically would reduce the pop but compromise optimal sound and should be avoided.
4. The position of the mic in relationship to the singer's mouth, as well as the way a singer grips the mic, effects two variables: the quality of the sound and the visual effect for the audience. The quality of the sound is the most important to consider;

is the mic being held at an angle and distance that allow for the best sound quality? If not, is it worth sacrificing quality of sound for visual effect. For example, a hip-hop singer might want the visual effect of holding the mic with a tight grip and horizontally. With some mics, this position could be fine, but with other mics it might compromise the sound. A jazz singer might want the cool, easy-going look of holding the mic at 45-degrees with just the fingertips. This position should allow for optimal quality of sound on all mics, however holding the mic with the fingertips might not be secure enough for some aggressive styles. Plan the mic position and grip style based on the needs of the genre. Avoid sacrificing sound quality unless absolutely necessary.

5. Instruct the singer to sing a phrase of a song as quietly as possible into the mic, creating an amplified but intimate sound. Ask the singer to repeat the phrase, increasing their loudness by 10% each time until they reach 90% of potential volume. If the singer varies the distance from lips to mic, make note of it and ask the singer to be conscious of this choice. Doing this exercise will help the singer understand the threshold of a microphone's input capabilities and how volume affects the sound coming out of the monitor.
6. Next, instruct the singer to sing the chorus of a song with maximum loudness variation. That is, sing some parts very, very quietly and other parts very loudly, making conscious decisions about mic location and angle to maximize the beauty or effectiveness of the interpretation. Repeat this several times until the adjustments become second nature for the singer.
7. Finally, ask the singer to sing their entire song with eyes closed and hearing focused on the sound coming out of the monitor. Their goal is to interpret the song with a variety of flavors for an artistic performance.

Using a microphone to enhance interpretation opens an astonishing palette of colors and intensities that aren't available to the unamplified singer. After the singer has achieved an artistic realization of their first song, challenge the singer to switch to a contrasting piece and develop an appropriate palate for the different opportunities in a new style.

RECIPE

# Inspired Inhalations!

*Kenneth Bozeman*

The vocal tract should be readied for singing before and during inhalation so that the singer can sing immediately without needing additional time or adjustments. Furthermore, the inhalation should be "inspired" by the expressive impulse to communicate. This will accomplish the time-honored "open throat" of the Italian school as long as we are not misled by the timbral distortion and false kinesthesia of the yawn sensation.

**INGREDIENTS:**
Noiseless Inhalation
Remapping the Throat Wall and Tongue Origin
Cooling in the Front
Expressive, Affective Motivation

**SERVES:**
All ages.

Along with appropriate training of the torso for respiration, effective pre-phonatory tuning of the vocal tract during inhalation prepares the singer for best function and outcome. This involves properly opening the throat with very light muscle poise. The simplest recipe for this "dish" takes advantage of our innate programming from the impulse to communicate.

Doing this well is challenged by our false kinesthesia for an open throat. What universally feels like an open throat is a "yawny [ɑ]." Conversely, an [i] vowel feels closed in the throat. Ironically, the opposite is the truth. Directing your singers to open their throats will likely invite this false response.

**Solutions:**

- Inhale with a helpful affect, such as inner amusement or mischief, or sincere empathy. The early Italian teachers advised the singer to "inhale through a smile, it opens the throat!" Genuine smiling is more about what you feel on the inside than about spreading your lips, but your face will reflect your expression. Try being very happy or pleased as you inhale and feel what that does to your throat and soft palate. It fronts your tongue and opens your throat.
- Realize that the back wall of your throat is always in front of your ears! It may feel further back if you are thinking of a yawn, but that sensation is really the sensation of your tongue backing up into your pharynx, something you don't want. When your throat is well opened—because your tongue is relaxed and fronted—your

throat ironically does not feel open and the back wall of your throat feels like it is in front of your ears, where it actually is!

- Your real tongue root—its attachment to your skeleton—is the inside back of your chin! Your tongue is round, folded over itself, and sits inside your jaw behind your chin. If you map it as if it originates at your larynx, that will back your tongue and narrow your throat. (See the image below) Mentally remap your tongue origin at the chin.
- When you inhale with a fronted tongue and opened throat, the inhalation will cool the front of your mouth—the tongue blade, front teeth and front hard palate. It will not cool your throat. The cooling of the wind chill effect is greatest where the vocal tract is the narrowest and the airspeed the fastest. We want that in the front, not the back.
- You can simply stay where you are to inhale—you don't need to overly open your mouth or reach forward for the air. Imagine a pleasant or an empathetic idea that you want to share with us. Let that impulse motivate your preparatory inhalation.
- Both the torso (chest and abdomen) and the vocal tract are tuned and poised by the impulse to communicate. Though it is certainly useful to know and rehearse the elements of good inhalation, this innate expressive programming—which we have right away at birth—organizes and coordinates voicing much better than any micro-managed, volitional process.

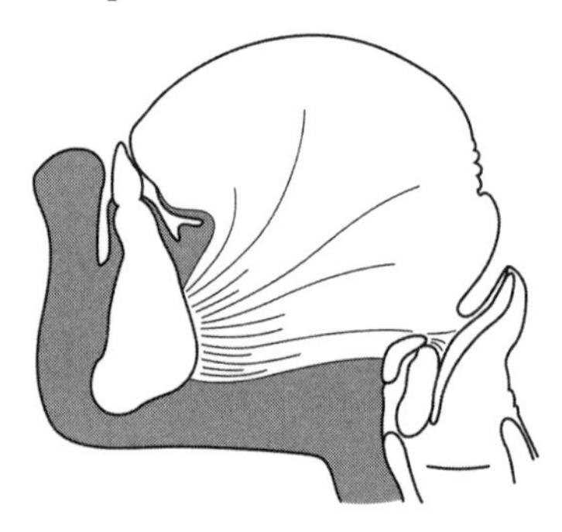

Tongue origin at the inside back of the chin

**Summary:**

- Be happy or empathetic!
- Keep the perceived distance from the lips to the back wall comfortably short.
- Mentally remap the back throat wall and the tongue shape and origin.
- Let a noiseless inhalation cool in the front, not in the back.

**Read More About It:**

Bozeman, Kenneth. "Remapping the Open Throat (Gola Aperta)." *Journal of Singing* 72, no. 2 (2015): 183–187.

Bozeman, Kenneth. *Practical Vocal Acoustics: Pedagogic Applications for Teachers and Singers*. Hillsdale, NY: Pendragon Press, 2013.

Bozeman, Kenneth. *Kinesthetic Voice Pedagogy: Motivating Acoustic Efficiency*. Gahanna, OH: Inside View Press, 2017.

RECIPE

# Planning the Menu for a Vocal Smorgasbord: Singing Across the Life Span

*Karen Brunssen*

Humans are the only creatures that sing with words. Acquisition of language and song begins with the birth cry of the newborn. As infants grow, the larynx descends, the tongue bends down into the throat, and the velum begins to move up and down better. Babbling is an infant's way of experimenting with melodic contour, new vowel shapes, and consonants. The shape of the torso changes from flared out cartilaginous ribs to boney ribs that no longer flare out. The lungs grow as millions of alveoli develop for exchange of oxygen and carbon dioxide. During adolescence, hormones suddenly trigger growth and change in every part of the body. The vocal tract, vocal folds, rib cage, and lungs all grow, but quite unsymmetrically. The younger support system is replaced with the mature support system that, along with grown-up vocal folds and a bigger vocal tract, is capable of phenomenal potential to sing. Considering the wonderful smorgasbord of every age in voice studios and ensembles, voice teachers and choral directors benefit if they know about the voice from birth through old age. It is not a one-size-fits-all, but rather different expectations and techniques at different points of development.

**INGREDIENTS:**
Methods and expectations for singing commensurate with age for babies, toddlers, children, adolescents, adults, and senescent singers.

**SERVES:**
This recipe is enough for all singers.

**The Menu:**
When planning a smorgasbord menu for grandchildren, cousins, siblings, parents, and grandparents, one must take into account the appetites and dietary restrictions of every person coming for dinner.

At the smorgasbord, **babies** will need parents to feed them. Their diet must be according to what they can swallow and digest without the benefit of teeth. Musical needs require help as well, via loving interaction with parents or caregivers that follows the lead of the baby. Babies cannot be force-fed, but rather, they do what they can do as they are able. Match pitches with them. If they make an "oo" face and a sound, imitate them as they admiringly look into your eyes. They love it when someone playfully helps them clap their hands or move their little legs while singing or listening to a song. If they cry, they are most comforted by the singing of their mothers.

**Toddlers** are very busy learning about everything around them, and seem to be messy, picky eaters. They would only eat macaroni and cheese and peanut butter sandwiches unless someone introduced new flavors to expand their "palate." Their musical appetites are similar. They are capable of receiving a lot of musical information if it is presented to them. Action songs with parents, grandparents, siblings, or cousins are perfect as they bring together rhythm, melodies, words, and movement. At first, they favor movement and rhythm over words and melody. Incrementally they put it all together.

Too often, we "cater" to the assumption that the diet of **children** is pizza, burgers, and hot dogs. We underestimate their ability to appreciate finer cuisine. Then one day we are surprised to notice that they like fish, broccoli, or green peppers. The same can be said about the vocal diet we present to children by way of repertoire. Some are just as capable of singing a Bach aria from a cantata as they are a Disney song, if we would just introduce that music to them. A child may discover they like singing activities that require them to read musical notation, make beautiful sounds with their voices, perform on stage, vigorously breathe and support their singing, and learn everything from the Beatles to Bach.

**Adolescents** are not very comfortable at smorgasbords. They seem preoccupied due to their own growth and change. Be sure to have a lot of food for the boys, because their appetites surge just as their hormones do. Girls become pickier about what they eat, are very aware of their surroundings, how they look, who they are with, and how very different from boys they are now. Boys' voices go down as girls' voices stay higher. The short boy turns into the 6' tall 12-year-old with a sort of raw singing voice that is an octave lower. The pudgy girl becomes a lanky teen with breathiness in her singing. This is evidence of a developmental "chink" between the vocal folds. Awkward vocalism is due to physical growth that outpaces adaption and coordination. It is normal! It merits the patience and persistence of voice teachers and choral directors in junior high, high school, and the first few years of college, who work with them as they "remap" how to sing after the hormonal surge of adolescence.

**Adults** want delicious, cutting-edge cuisine, with red wine to go with red meat, white wine with fish or chicken, a beer with a burger, and the spicier, the better. The very fashionable "small plates" allow for a little bit of everything, with vibrant, rich, bold flavors matched with the perfect wine. For the next 30–40 years, adults may pursue many culinary options in their singing lives. There is a wide variety of interesting vocal genres, styles, and languages. Perhaps they will be the "chef" who starts their own singing organization, teaching studio, or contributes to cutting-edge scholarship about singing. Hormones are generally stable. Body shape and strength is at its peak. Vocal technique has revealed their voices to them. They can sing as little or as much as their aptitude, talent, energies, and desires go. They can give it their all for a career, or as a compliment to other careers.

**Senescence** is a time when spicy, hot food is not tolerated as well. Culinary preferences necessarily change in order to maintain digestive health. Senescence singing requires maintenance as the muscles of support, lungs, and vocal folds lose elasticity and strength. Residual volume in the lungs increases, which means there is less air that can go in and less air that can go out, so you have to do the most you can with what you have. A mindful vocal diet, that keeps the muscles of breathing in shape, and includes semi-occluded vocal tract exercises, can go a long way in senescence vocal habilitation.

**Summary**
The great thing about smorgasbords is that food is professionally prepared so the culinary desires of everyone invited is included. There is a wide variety of delicious foods to select according to different appetites. The culinary creativity, training, knowledge, skills, and methods of preparation needed for those who work with a full palate of singers across the "vocal smorgasbord" merits a firm, factual foundation.

RECIPE

# Recipe for Developing an Opera Quality

*Terry Chasteen*

Before you begin, know that this recipe is intended for post-pubescent aged "cooks," and is not for the impatient, nor is it a recipe with which one should ever become truly, 100% satisfied. Mastery of the recipe will require a continual striving for improvement by carefully adjusting the ingredients. Finally, it is best to never begin this process completely on your own, but rather under the supervision of an experienced "master chef," if you will, that you trust and who will be committed to advise the repetition of the recipe until your desired result can be repeated independently.

**INGREDIENTS:**
Healthy, energetic, and enthusiastic person with:

- 1 tall, balanced skeletal structure, including all bones and musculature
- 1 skull, balanced freely at the top of the spine, BRAIN included, and in good working order
- 1 jaw (relaxed from its hinges)
- 1 tongue (relaxed forward into the jaw and free of tension)[1]
- 1 vocal tract (pharyngeal space, oral space, and lips included) freely prepared for vowel shaping
- 1 larynx (gently lowered, thyroid portion tilting forward over the cricoid, and containing healthy vocal folds)[2]
- 1 velum, raised
- 1 respiratory system (lungs, diaphragm working freely)
- 1 torso, musculature ready for energetically free movement

**SERVES:**
Those singers who have completed puberty and have a desire to produce an operatic quality with their voices.

Have singers start combining the ingredients as follows after predetermining a pitch you would like to produce and the vowel sound(s) through which you would like to produce it.

1 A variation could be to help the tongue move purposely forward in the mouth with the tip gently pressing against the bottom teeth.

2 For the experienced cook, one ingredient not mentioned in the recipe, but which can have some affect, is the ***Aryepiglottic sphincter***. It might be placed in the list between the vocal tract and lowered larynx. Use of this partial closure of the epiglottis and muscles at the top of the larynx, just at the bottom of the pharyngeal cavity can have an acoustic effect on the vibration as this space narrows slightly.

1. Begin, through inhalation, to engage the respiratory system into a full and free expansion. As the diaphragm lowers, one should experience the release and expansion of the abdominal muscles of the lower torso and the expansion of the rib cage in the upper torso, remembering that one is a three-dimensional being, not just a front, back, or side, yet encompassing all of these.
2. Simultaneously:
   a. Release the jaw at its hinges allowing it to comfortably lower.
   b. Allow the tip of the tongue to remain gently cradled against the bottom front teeth.
   c. Allow the velum to be in a lifted, high position.
   d. Move the larynx into its comfortably, lowered position with the thyroid cartilage tilted forward over the cricoid cartilage.
   e. Allow the vocal tract to form the shape of your favorite vowel, with lips relaxed open and their corners free.

   (CAUTION! With some vowel shapes the tongue may want to slide backward into the vocal tract or be subconsciously retracted. Care should be taken to insure this does not occur. In lowering the larynx trust the tiny muscles below it to accomplish this and definitely DO NOT rely upon the tongue for this. You will have to trust that the described muscles are where they are despite the fact you will not be able to feel them working.)
3. With the air at the ready, think the predetermined pitch, and engage the vocal folds in the larynx by beginning to release air. This thought is enough for the brain to signal the vocal folds to move together into the position for the predetermined pitch frequency.
4. Engage the muscles of the upper and lower torso with enough energy to not collapse onto the lungs and allow the diaphragm to begin its upward movement. This will send air upward, creating pressure that will build beneath the vocal folds, and finally be released then pulling the folds back together again at an alarmingly fast rate that is almost incomprehensible! Thus begins the vibratory process that produces the pitch!
5. Now, allow the vibration to radiate upward and through the prepared vocal tract while keeping the torso energy constant to support the pressure inside the comfortably low and stable larynx, and to sustain the pitch. Moving through the vocal tract, the vibration will amplify as it moves through the space. Allow the vibration to strike along the bony structure of the skull as well as radiate, as it can, through the chest cavity. All this will help to further amplify the vibration. As the torso energy increases, so will the intensity of the vibration being resonated. Adjust until you have the desired volume being certain that the velum remains high and the thyroid tilted.

You are now releasing a tone in opera quality! You are ready to experiment with sustaining the quality; first in simple vocalise exercises, and when those are comfortable, into repertoire!

RECIPE

# A *Consommé* of Consonants

*Steven R. Chicurel-Stein*

Merriam Webster defines *consommé* as "clear soup made from well-seasoned stock." How often have composers, lyricists, coaches, conductors—and audiences—hoped to gain meaning and joy from a vocal performance, only to experience it as a garbled gumbo of sounds? While the importance of vowel production to verbal intelligibility and singing cannot be understated, the vocalist who gives equal importance to consonants will be best equipped to produce a "vocal *consommé*" in which the "stock" of vowels and consonants combine to deliver most clearly the sounds and meanings intended by creator and interpreter alike.

**INGREDIENTS:**
Larynx
Articulators
Active listeners
Consonants and vowels

**SERVES:**
The composer and lyricist, the listener, and the vocalist.

While vocal lines consist of many elements, three fundamental aspects are pitch, rate, and duration. Pitch is the note-by-note path dictated by the composer; rate is tempo, also mandated in the score (but understood to have its own variability, as we know one person's *allegro* will never precisely match that of another). That leaves only one variable at our disposal—duration—and this is the aspect of vocal production in which consonants and vowels exist in relation to each other.

In singing, vowels "carry" a melodic line. In doing so, it becomes easy—and understandable—to distort the importance of, and balance between, consonants and vowels. An over-emphasis on vowels results in a lack of intelligibility and consequently, the meaning of words is diminished, if not lost. Additionally, we have all experienced singing and acting teachers, along with choral conductors, admonishing their charges to "put on those final consonants," but why is the last consonant the only one that counts?

Consonants serve as unique building blocks to words and their importance stretches beyond mere meaning: consonants are a source of great emotive potential. In fact, one may easily support the notion that information conveyed in consonants provides the listener with more meaning—emotion, context—than vowels. Although, as the science of sound and acoustics reveal much about the threshold of hearing with regards to sound duration, a listener's distance from the sound source, and the minimum amplitude of a sound perceived by the human ear, non-scientists can understand this complex of ideas with a simple demonstration.

In my voice class, I have students speak a word or phrase with the purpose of expressing different, pre-determined meanings. We can then examine and articulate facets of that speaking experience resulting in the (successful) conveyance of the intended meaning. Here are three examples using the utterance of my name, Steve:

- **Surprise/shock:** "Steve" is short in overall duration. The initial /s/ is vocalized quite quickly and loudly. The silence before the /t/ is long. The amplitude of the /t/ is higher than the vowel that follows. The vowel /i/ is likewise short. The final /v/, while lower in amplitude than the initial /st/ combination is a prominent feature of the utterance.
- **"You rascal, you!":** The /s/ is lengthened. There's a decrescendo that leads to the silence before the /t/ is uttered. Another silence precedes the /i/. The onset of the /i/ is glottal. The /i/ is uttered on a singular pitch and is shorter than the consonant group that preceded it. The final /v/ is lengthened to a duration that nearly matches the /i/. Finally, there is a slight crescendo on the voicing of the /v/ as it's sustained.
- **"Do that again!":** (I include this option so that students realize in some cases, the characteristics of a vowel change along with those of consonants). The /s/ is longer than in the previous example. There is less silence before the burst of the /t/ followed by a smooth onset of the /i/ (as opposed to glottal or aspirate). In this interpretation, the /i/ becomes prominent. It is longer in time, and the "melody" of the inner-vowel lilt provides color and meaning. Likewise, the final /v/ is longer.

The preceding examples beg the question, "That's fine in speech, but how do I do this in singing?" It's quite possible; since vowels will still typically occur *on* the beat, consonants must occur *before* the beat, on the upbeat. My experience helping singers understand and prioritize their focus on consonant production has demonstrated that if performers first and foremost want to fully serve the composer's and lyricist's intentions (and maximize engagement and meaning for the listener), then creating a masterful vocal *consommé* where consonants are fully, if not differently valued as vowels, will be the chef's best recipe for success.

RECIPE

# Online Voice Teaching: Serve Up Your Teaching Across the World!

*Mindy Damon*

Do you want to cook up a double or triple batch of your tried and true vocal technique recipe to serve more students by expanding the reach of your teaching beyond the walls of your voice studio? This addition to your recipe may just please your technique-hungry crowd!

**INGREDIENTS:**
A solid teaching pedagogy
A willingness to be open to technology use
A Smartphone and laptop with internet access (for both you and your online student)
Pre-recorded vocal exercises and accompaniment
Real-time visual feedback software (Sing and See Software™ by Cantovation is recommended)
Video Conferencing app (Zoom™ is recommended)

**SERVES:**
Vocal technique to students who would otherwise not be under your instruction.

It is likely that there are aspiring voice students out there who would benefit from your teaching, but live too far away to commute to your studio. This format may be used consistently for online students or occasionally for residential student when it is impossible to meet face-to-face for such events as maternity leave, vacations, illness, or travel.

Research shows that family obligations, careers, touring, or financial hardships are factors that keep students and teachers disconnected for regular, systematic training.[1] Lessening the worries of travel, traffic, and parking can relieve your student's mind of stress, and provide clarity of mind for the learning process. This aspect aligns with Sweller's (1970) Cognitive Load Theory for optimal student learning in that the removal of distractions can simplify the learning process and prepare the mind to absorb a healthy heaping of good teaching.

**Instructions:**

1. Set aside pre-conceived ideas concerning this format and add some research of the literature. While other fields have been receptive to online education, music educa-

1 Timothy Braun, "Making a choice: The Perceptions and Attitudes of Online Graduate Students," *Journal of Technology and Teacher Education* 16, no. 1 (2008): 63–92.

tors have been more resistant to this platform.[2] Skepticism abounds concerning the viability of online voice teaching, yet research shows that this format yields efficacy and student-teacher connection similar to that of face-to-face lessons, and that students appreciate the convenience of the online format.[3]

2. Gather all ingredients for yourself and require all online students to secure internet access, hardware, and software.
3. Measure your openness to use of new technology. Dye states that this format can "bring any teacher into contact with any student who seeks their guidance and instruction, provided technology limitations can be met and successfully negotiated."[4]
4. Add a video conferencing app such as Zoom™ and real-time visual feedback such as Sing and See™ (Cantovation) to your laptop and smartphone. Your student must download the Zoom™ app and add you as a contact for easiest connection when it is lesson time.
5. Measure your internet connection with prospective online students and explore the software prior to the first lesson. Grind out any technical bugs you may be experiencing until all components blend to yield a smooth consistency.
6. All accompaniment must be pre-recorded or downloaded in advance of the lesson so that your student can sing along with accompaniment played on one device (ex. a laptop with speakers), while using a second device (ex. a smartphone) for face-to-face contact with you.
7. When it is time for the lesson, contact your student via video conferencing (such as Zoom™). During the lesson, keep real-time visual feedback (Sing and See™) running on your laptop. Share your screen so that your student will be able to see your face and real-time visual feedback as well. Real-time visual feedback can facilitate deeper learning as it provides an internalization of the vocal concepts as related to pitch accuracy, tone clarity, and stabilization of vibrato by allowing the student to see his or her voice movement in the moment.[5] Further, by sharing your screen, you are both able to see the same vocal analysis at the same time.

The teacher maintains the position of the master, as established in the time-honored master-apprentice model. The traditionally strong bond between voice teacher and student need not be forfeited in the online environment. Research demonstrates that relationships forged in the online environment can be quite robust and carry a strong sense of connection.[6] With the availability of ever-improving technology in a field that used to be limited by proximity, why not remove the issue of distance from those who might grow under your tried and true teaching? Consider garnishing your expertise with the expansion of an online format.

2 Fred J. Rees, "Distance Learning and Collaboration in Music Education," in *The New Handbook of Research in Music Education*, eds. R. Colwell & C. Richardson (New York: Oxford University Press, 2002).

3 Richard J. Dammers, "Utilizing Internet-based Videoconferencing for Instrumental Music Lessons," *MENC: The National Association for Music Education* 28, no. 1 (2009): 17–24.

4 Keith Dye. "Student and Instructor Behaviors in Online Music Lessons: An Exploratory Study." *International Journal of Music Education* 34, no. 2 (2016): 163.

5 Jean Callaghan, William Thorpe, and Jan van Doorn. "The Science of Singing and Seeing," in *Proceedings of the Conference of Interdisciplinary Musicology* (CIM04), eds. R. Parncutt, A. Kessler, and F. Zimmer (Graz, Austria, 2004): 15–18.

6 Lun Zhang and Jonathan H. Zhu, "Regularity and Variability: Growth Patterns of Online Friendships," *International Journal of Web Services Research* 11, no. 4 (2014): 19–31.

RECIPE

# Too Much Noise in the Kitchen

*James F. Daugherty*

Excessive levels of cumulative noise exposure, including exposure to self- or other-produced vocal sounds, may contribute to noise-induced hearing loss, an irreversible impairment. Voice teachers can reduce noise exposures through understanding and proactive prevention.

**INGREDIENTS:**
An ounce of prevention
A cup of attention to studio room environment
A dash of scheduling savvy

**SERVES:**
Voice teachers and students.

Noise induced hearing loss (NIHL) entails a permanent threshold shift (NIPTS) in higher frequencies (3–6 kHz) due to destruction of sensory cells in the inner ear. NIHL develops cumulatively over a long period of time. However, even a noise-induced temporary threshold shift (NITTS) following short-term exposures to high sound levels can lead to a permanent loss of sensory input for up to 50% of auditory nerve fibers in the high-frequency region of the cochlea.

Data from some recent noise dosimetry studies illustrate why voice teachers may have cause for concern:

- Some solo singers exceeded, in one individual practice session, the permissible all-day noise dose suggested by The National Institute of Occupational Safety and Health (NIOSH). These singers also acquired higher doses than some solo players of brass and woodwind instruments during individual practice sessions.[1]
- The two-day average noise dose acquired by some other solo singers, solely during individual practice sessions, exceeded 114% of NIOSH allowed daily dose.[2]
- Acquired noise doses for university voice instructors teaching a single, 1-hr lesson ranged from 7%–85% of NIOSH permissible daily dose. Instructors teaching two, contiguous 1-hr lessons acquired doses ranging from 23%–210%. Teaching three, contiguous 1-hr lessons yielded noise doses ranging from 28%–81%. One instruc-

1 Nilesh J. Washnik, Susan L. Phillips, and Sandra Teglas, "Student's music exposure: Full-day personal dose measurements," *Noise & Health* 18, no. 81, (2016): 98–103.

2 Kieren H. Smith, Tracianne B. Neilsen, and Jeremy Grimshaw, "Full-day Noise Exposure for Student Musicians at Brigham Young University," *Acoustical Society of America: Proceedings of Meetings on Acoustics 30*, no. 1, (2017): 035002.

tor who taught four, contiguous 1-hr lessons in a single afternoon acquired 290% of her permissible daily dose during that timeframe. Two voice instructors wore dosimeters during waking hours for one day. The male instructor acquired 1100%, or eleven times, the permissible daily noise dosage. The female instructor acquired 1500%, or fifteen times, her daily allowed dose.[3]

Numerous variables contribute to acquired noise exposures. In the studio, the level and duration of vocal output power (which can vary according to repertoire, vocal style employed, and "size" of vocal instrument), room reverberation rate, room dimensions, presence of piano or another instrumental accompaniment, number of lessons taught, relative percentages of singing vs. conversational times during lessons, and time devoted to one's own practice each contribute to a voice teacher's daily noise exposure. Outside the studio, various activities, including rehearsals and performances in other venues, driving, mowing the lawn, teaching other classes, or attending meetings and sports events, add to one's cumulative exposure.

To be proactive in protecting hearing acuity, consider the following:

- Schedule a baseline hearing assessment from an audiologist.
- Consider occasionally wearing a noise dosimeter. There are several affordable dosimeter options today. Although not research grade, these options nonetheless help in identifying those teaching situations in which you tend to acquire higher noise doses.
- Take inventory of your studio environment and, as possible, make modifications. Research suggests that, depending upon configuration and construction materials, smaller rooms or studios can yield higher noise exposures than larger spaces. The intensity of received sound is inversely proportional to the square of the distance from the sound source (Inverse Square Law). Larger rooms can enable increased distance between teachers, students, and pianos. Higher room reverberation rates contribute to noise exposure more than rooms with lesser reverberation rates. Although research indicates that singers prefer more reverberant over "dry" room acoustics, excessive reverberation can be addressed by the addition of curtains, wall tapestries, or carpet. Assess also whether teacher or student is near a source of ambient noise, such as that from an HVAC duct. Research demonstrates that singers tend unconsciously to increase vocal output power in the presence of masking noises (Lombard Effect).
- Plan. Consider potential noise exposures as you schedule daily activities. For example, if you know you will engage in longer duration practice or performance, or attend a rock concert or basketball game, teaching numerous voice lessons that same day may not be advisable.
- Consider wearing hearing protection. Because voice teachers' ears serve as a primary means of diagnosing and correcting student performance, and the perceived amplitude of students' higher frequency partials figure prominently in such diagnoses, wearing hearing protection during voice lessons may not be desirable. However, voice teachers could well don hearing protection for other daily activities.
- Discuss proactive conservation of hearing acuity with your voice students.

Our voices can recover from some forms of fatigue with voice rest. Our auditory structures, by contrast, do not fully recover even from short-term exposures to excessive noise.

3 James F. Daugherty, Heather R. Nelson, Amelia A. Rollings, Melissa L. Grady, and S. Thomas Scott, "Noise Doses Acquired by University Singing Voice Instructors Across One Week in Studio Teaching Environments," (in press, 2017).

RECIPE

# Structuring an Independent Vocal Warm-Up: A Recipe for Successful Growth

*Kristin Dauphinais*

So often teachers send students off to practice with the assumption that they know what to do. However, once in that tiny cell, staring at the piano, many students struggle with how to warm-up the voice. Some will do thirty seconds of humming and think they are ready to go. While others may jump immediately to vocal pyrotechnics of Olympic proportions. The following recipe is a guide to help singers begin their practice sessions in a healthy manner aimed at consistent technical development.

Preheat the entire body to stretched, warm and focused.

**INGREDIENTS:**

| | |
|---|---|
| 5 minutes | Breathing and focusing exercises (may be combined with pre-heat) |
| 5–10 minutes | Easy vocal warm-ups |
| 10–15 minutes | Registration balancing, vowel clarity, and legato exercises |
| 5–10 minutes | Range extension and agility |
| Dash | Special skills practice as needed (trills, voiced consonants, *messa di voce*, or other technique goals not covered above) |

* Vocal needs are highly variable from day-to-day. Adjust timings as necessary.

**SERVES:**
All singers.

Prior to any good practice session, the body must be warmed-up and the singer must be in a positive, growth-focused state of mind. This can be achieved by a quick walk around the building, or other favorite exercise designed to get the blood flowing and body released of tension. Physical needs will vary by time of day, stress level, or fatigue, and the amount of physical warm-up required for this portion will be directly correlated to these conditions. The body is the foundation of healthy singing, if the body is not prepared, tension and/or lack of focus will plague the practice session.

Next, attention must go to the breath. Favorite exercises that quiet the breath, stretch the intercostal muscles, focus on diaphragmatic breathing, or extend the length of an exhalation can be inserted. Breathing exercises may be combined with continued physical warm-ups by stretching or moving at the same time. Use this time to quiet the mind and come into focus for the coming tasks.

Once the breath is grounded, the voice must be warmed up in a gentle, easy manner. Vocalises that involve humming, lip-trills, or an alternation of humming and simple vowels in the mid-voice may be used. Simple descending five note scales on a "hum" or with an alternation of the "hum" and [a] are some of my favorite places to start. Even at this early stage, attention to legato will enhance technical development. Keeping the sound fluid without making a pitch change is challenging for most. From here, the singer can open into vowel-based vocalises, i.e., [u–o–i–e–a] on the same descending five note scale. These should start simple, in a comfortable range, and then extend into exercises that balance the registers and even out production. The focus for this section should be on keeping the quality of the resonance even throughout the range, maintaining vowel clarity, freedom of production, and legato. This is an excellent time for the singer to record, listen back to themselves, and attempt exercises again for improvement. A recording app on a smart phone can be a great 21st century tool for growth and gaining feedback. When the voice feels supple and aligned, proceed to agility.

Agility work is important for all voice types in order to maintain the flexibility in a healthy instrument. Beginners can master coloratura exercises that span a third or fifth and more advanced singers can cover an octave or even two. The focus for this section should be on maintaining the integrity of the vowel, freedom of production, clarity, and an even precise tempo. (Note: range or speed should not exceed technical prowess.) Once the full range is pliable and energized, the singer may add a pinch of special skills such as trills, *messa di voce*, or octave leaps, particularly if they are related to technical or repertoire goals. This is also an excellent time to transition into literature by addressing challenging portions as a vocalise. For example, that tricky triplet section of a Handel run can be separated out and repeated at various pitch levels to gain fluency, or a difficult leap to a pianissimo high note can be practiced in a more comfortable tessitura and then gradually transposed to the written range.

Following the completion of the warm-up, the singer should be ready to transition into specific repertoire goals and continue their healthy and productive practice session.

RECIPE

# Voices in Transition: A Recipe for Selecting Appropriate Choral Literature

*Rollo Dilworth*

Perhaps one of the most pervasive challenges for all those who lead a vocal ensemble is repertoire selection. Given that voice changes can begin as early as the upper elementary grades and continue well past the high school years, it is likely that choral teachers at every level will encounter voices that are in transition. The purpose of this recipe is to offer some guiding principles for choosing (and modifying) standard voicings of choral literature for young singers.

**INGREDIENTS:**
Any vocal ensemble with singers whose voices are in transition.
Selected choral literature ranging from Unison to SATB.

**SERVES:**
All ensembles with voices in transition and those who lead them.

**Technical Questions to ask when choosing choral literature:**

1. What types of voicings should I consider using for my ensemble if there are singers whose voices are changing?
2. How can I ensure that the choral scores I choose will adequately accommodate the vocal needs of my singers?

Each and every voice in your ensemble is unique. Each voice, regardless of gender, will come to your rehearsal each day with its own set of strengths as well as opportunities for growth. The amount of expansion, contraction, and shifting of vocal ranges in your ensemble will be abundant and diverse—making it seem nearly impossible to find repertoire that will suit the needs of each and every student.

Maintaining accurate knowledge of each singer's vocal range is important. Periodically check each singer's range, maintain an accurate record of vocal changes, and maintain an open dialogue with singers to collaborate on strategies for success. While this can be challenging and time consuming, knowing this information will enable you to assign the appropriate vocal line, and correctly position the singer within the ensemble where they can systematically develop both their voices and musicianship, and ultimately, do their best work. Creating a successful choral experience for singers in vocal transition will require the appropriate mix of repertoire. For every vocal ensemble, the ideal recipe of repertoire voicings may be different. Below are the possibilities. Choose the mix of voicings that best match the needs of your singers.

**Repertoire Recipes and Considerations:**

1. **Unison music**
   Developing a good unison sound is certainly one of the basic principles of choral singing. Listening skills, sight-singing skills, intonation, blend, vowel unification, vocal color, resonance, breath management, and phrasing are among the numerous concepts that can be more cultivated and refined when only one vocal line is involved. Voices that are changing may struggle with singing unison in the written octave.
   Therefore, when selecting unison music, check the score to see if the accompaniment will support the possibility of singers who need to drop down an octave. If this is the case, then allow those transitioning singers to sing down the octave in those segments of the music where it is comfortable
2. **Two-Part (SA) music**
   Two-part music, written for treble voices, offers an available option for male voices that are developing a lower range extension, and for female voices that are undergoing a temporary reduction in range. What is labeled as "Part II" or "Alto" in the score can benefit both male and female voices in transition. Emerging baritones are likely able to sing "Part II" down the octave, while female voices with limited range can sing the part as written.
3. **SSA (3-part treble)/SSAA (4-part treble) music**
   If you choose this type of voicing for your maturing mixed gender choral ensemble, check the vocal lines carefully to make sure the alto part(s) is/are low enough to accommodate those emerging tenor and baritone voices. Especially look for pieces with low A's, G's and even F's below middle C.
4. **Three-part mixed music**
   Most three-part mixed music will work for boys whose voices have not dropped and who do not have male voice *passaggio* issues (often D–F above middle C). These boys with unchanged voices can sing moderate alto and tenor lines without issue. If you have a few boys whose voices are expanding down into the baritone and bass ranges, then look for three-part mixed music that offers alternative lower notes to accommodate these voices.
5. **SAB music**
   Although the ranges of the bass parts will accommodate more fully developed bass singers, emerging tenor voices and cambiatas will struggle to sing these vocal lines. For tenor voices, you may need to look for part-shifting opportunities in which they sing the alto part in places where it is low enough for them and then shift to the bass/baritone part when it is high enough for them.
6. **SATB music**
   This option works well for an ensemble that consists of diverse vocal ranges. As the male and female voices undergo shifts in singing range, it is good to find SATB pieces that have the following properties:
   - occasional unison treble (soprano, alto) and lower (tenor, bass) voice lines;
   - occasional sharing of vocal line for alto and tenor voice lines;
     - both scenarios allow for support between sections and strengt mance of vocal line.
   - modest vocal ranges;
     - bass/baritone: A to middle C
     - tenor: F to F

- alto: middle C to F
- soprano: middle C to F
- occasional and cautious extensions of up to a 3rd on either side

- minimum number of vocal patterns that keep singers in the bridge points between registers (*passaggio*).

Keep in mind that it will be challenging to find a piece of choral music that will be "perfect" for every singer in an ensemble where voices are in transition. The goal is to be aware of each singer's situation, and to make literature choices that offer the kinds of flexibility needed in order for your singers to be successful.

RECIPE

# The Plain Cookie: Overcoming the Myth of the Female Vocal "Break"

*Kate Duncan*

Every cookie starts with the same base: fat, protein, some form of grain starch, a little salt, and a whole lot of sugar. Until we start sprinkling nutmeg or chocolate chips into the batter, it could be any type of cookie! Consider your core vocal tone as this plain cookie, whereas the "spices" are flips, melismas, growls, and even genre-specific stylization. The goal of the singer should be to root their core vocal sound in this healthy "batter." Imagine a cookie built on nothing but spices and Reeses' candies—without its batter base, it's an overwhelming mess of angular flavors. The same can be said for singers who use those vocal "spices" as their foundational grounds. This recipe aims to strip away those ornamental spices, thereby fortifying the batter.

**INGREDIENTS:**
Stacked and aligned body mechanics
The ability to think in opposites
Healthy dollop of imagination
Desire to create one single vocal instrument throughout one's range

**SERVES:**
Seekers of core vocal tone, or "the plain cookie:" the seamlessness between the tone/timbre of the notes in the lower voice and the upper voice. This recipe serves as a jumping off point towards converging and unifying those timbres into one vocal instrument.

As a young college vocalist studying both classical and jazz styles, I was keenly aware of a disjunct timbre throughout my range. The notes in my lower range sounded lush and resonant, while my higher notes contained a clear, edgy ping. The middle, though, sometimes sounded fuzzy or weak, and other notes simply flipped from one timbre into another, as if a completely "other" singer inhabited my body from one register to the next, sounding like three different humans at once!

I was also surrounded by terms like "lower and upper register," "*passaggio*," and the worst of them: "the break." As I deepened my studies, my eyes were finally opened to the concept of a unified vocal instrument.

To create that healthy neutral vocal timbre in students and ourselves, the solution is two-fold:

**Step One: Terminology**

1. Clean up pedagogical language. Acknowledging the schismatic effect terms like "head voice," "chest voice," "break," "bridge," and even "*passaggio*," might have, calls attention to some of the divisions conjured by these dangerously false images of two items needing something additional to hinge them together as one. Eventually, the singer will think of themselves as a unified instrument, not just a sum of their vocal parts.
   The majority of vocal training begins with mental conception that begets a physical execution of sound. Thus, it is imperative to use language that causes singers to think of themselves as one instrument, capable of innumerable colors, timbres, and styles! Think of how silly it would be to talk about the tonal timbre and production of one's left hand versus one's right hand while playing the piano. Although some notes are low and some are high, they all come from the same instrument. Vocalizing is no different.

Singers can move to the second step once they are accustomed to vocalizing as one instrument. The goal is to create a grounded, "tone-forward" sound, meaning the core of the sound will feel as if it is placed in the front of your mouth, emanating forward of the soft-palate. Often, jazz and contemporary singers struggle with the middle of their tone by creating an unnatural "break" in the middle of their register from resonating too far back in the mechanism, creating a false sense of being in tune because it rattles the small bones in one's ears. Once the notes reach the middle of their range in this positioning, though; the requisite switch of placement needed is so dramatic that it creates a "breaking" sound, and a distinct change in timbre. In combination with semi- occluded vocal tract exercises, the following imagery exercise, in step two, can be used to ground the singer to their tone and unify their sound.

**Step Two: Stirring the Batter**

1. With a forward vocalization in mind, stand with a well-aligned, stacked posture.
2. Sing an ascending octave major scale, which contains the pitches: Bb3, B3, and C4, on the syllable "loo."
3. As you sing, imagine two *large* copper vats at both your left and right sides filled with cookie batter needing to be stirred as you sing up the scale. Envision the tension a thick batter creates against large stirring paddles, grounding your tone to that exterior tension (be careful not to embody that tension in the throat!). The gooey batter's "push-back" from the stirring causes the baker/singer to bend their knees and engage their quadriceps in creating the torque necessary to fully mix the ingredients, so you should do the same!

Using forward placement and this antithetical, grounding imagery, the singer is able to establish connection in body to tone, working against the natural, yet counterproductive inclination to strain their bodies too high or too tall while ascending up through their range. The singer eventually notices strengthened previously weak points in their range, and a unified intonation throughout.

RECIPE

# Everything but the Kitchen Sink: Singing in All Styles

*Rosana Eckert*

Vocal versatility, the ability to sing authentically in a variety of styles, is a beneficial trait in today's music market. Singers who have broad stylistic abilities are able to participate in a broad range of performance opportunities and expand their musical network. Is it possible to sing with a classical choral approach one day and an edgy pop sound the next day? Yes. With a solid understanding of vocal technique and a thoughtful approach to preparation, a vocalist can condition their voice for technical and stylistic versatility. It's all about cross-training, deep listening, and imitation.

**INGREDIENTS:**
Access to a large collection of stylistically varied musical recordings
A good ear for detail
A willingness to imitate and experiment
An understanding of vocal registers, vocal fold compression, and resonance
A daily vocal routine for developing strength and consistency in various techniques

**SERVES:**
All singers who want to increase their vocal versatility.

To sing authentically in a variety of styles, a singer must do two things: develop an understanding of the technique, style, and overall delivery approach associated with each genre, and develop the mastery and versatility of vocal technique to be able to reproduce the various sounds.

## Understanding the Style

Just like learning a language, the best way to master a new singing style is to listen and imitate. To begin this process, have the singer find a recording of a vocal artist singing in a style they would like to learn. Choosing an artist with a similar singing range is best, but various software programs can raise and lower the key of a recording, allowing the singer to imitate a song outside of their natural range. Listen to this recording together several times, and analyze the following singing elements:

- Timing of the lyrics (phrasing)
- Dynamics and overall volume of the performance
- Use of vibrato and straight tone (if there is vibrato, analyze the speed, width, and intensity)
- Embellishments and overall style (scoops, slides, extra melody notes or licks, onset, etc.)

- Tonal approach (chest voice vs. head voice or blending registers, round/dark sound, forward/bright sound, buzzing/covered sound—try to get an idea of soft palate lift and oral cavity space needed to reproduce the sound)
- Vocal fold compression (breathy/light tone, balanced or focused tone, pressed/tight tone)
- Diction style and overall energy of articulators (mouth opening, lyric "chewing," approach to diphthongs, conversational or affected diction vs. formal diction, etc.)

Choose a section of the recording on which to focus. Begin with the first two measures of that section. Have the singer sing along with the recording softly, imitating each of the analyzed elements. Once learned, have the singer try to match the perceived volume of the artist. Next, record the singer a cappella, singing the excerpt without the model recording, and have them listen back. This is the best way for the singer to hear their imitation accuracy. Take note: the less familiar the singer is with the style on the recording, the longer it will take them to master the imitation.

When they feel confident with the first two measures, have the singer go on to the second two measures and repeat the process. Continue to add measures, one or two at a time, until the entire section is done. Again, this could take minutes, hours, days, or even longer if these are new skills for their voice. Depending on the type of song the singer is imitating, it may not be necessary for them to learn the entire song in order to grasp the style concepts. Help them set reasonable goals, and remind them that it's better to do a small section with exceptional accuracy than a longer section with inaccuracies. Set the imitation standards high, and help troubleshoot technique when the match is not right.

**Developing the Technique**

Having a solid understanding of vocal technique is important when bouncing from style to style.

It is particularly important to understand vocal registers (chest/speech register and head/falsetto register), and how to isolate them and blend them together in various ways. Men sing primarily in chest register in all styles, using some head voice or blending of registers as they ascend. Women typically speak in chest register and sing in chest, head, or a blending of the two. Pop style singers tend to bring chest voice high into their head register while classical singers tend to bring head voice down into their speech register. Blending the two registers together in various ways is found in all styles.

Be sure singers warm up prior to vocal exercise. Help them develop a daily vocal exercise routine, working both chest and head register with vibrato and straight tone. Have singers work each register separately, women aiming to build chest voice strength to at least a Bb4 (above middle C), men building chest strength to at least an F4 (above middle C). They should use as little throat tension as possible, taking care not to let the larynx ride up and squash the sound as they ascend. Rather, singers should stay relaxed in the throat and let the feeling of resonance travel upward. When working head voice/falsetto separately, men and women should try to stay in head voice until at least middle C, building toward purity of tone. Work on blending the two registers in various ways. While in chest voice, singers can engage the primary head voice muscle (cricothyroid) in varying degrees by easing the vocal fold compression (releasing tension) as they ascend. While in head voice, singers can engage the primary chest voice muscle (thyroarytenoid) by adding some vocal fold compression or a feeling of grounding from below. Experiment with vibrato and straight tone throughout the process. There are many resources available for exploring mixed voice and vibrato. If these concepts are new to singers, have them explore!

Lastly, have singers experiment with the size and direction of their tone. Have them lift the soft palate (at the back of the throat) by yawning or pretending to pop their ears, as if on an airplane. Have them sing with the soft palate lifted to varying degrees and see how that changes the sound. Have singers experiment with the direction of the tone by aiming the sound at the front teeth, the roof of the mouth, and the back of the throat. As they imitate each artist, help them figure out the vocal "setting" needed to reproduce the artist's sound. Singers should stay aware of their vocal health throughout the process. Not every recording artist sings with efficient technique, so some imitations might be too "costly." Be sure they look for the most efficient ways to achieve the sounds they want.

RECIPE

# Finding the Ingredients Towards Yummy, Unusual Tastes: Extra-Normal Voice

*Michael Edward Edgerton*

Exploring new sounds are to the singer, as new tastes are to the chef. By working with new combinations of ingredients, the singer becomes the master chef of their new creation. Not all pastries taste the same, nor do all voices sound the same. Therefore, it will be shown that each singer already has at their fingertips, a multitude of ways to develop new performance technique, just as a chef has in creating new cuisine from already existing ingredients.

**INGREDIENTS:**
A voice
An interest in new techniques
A desire to explore new types of expressions
A good set of ears
Ability to concentrate

**SERVES:**
Solo and ensemble voices; desire to explore new expressions and techniques; singing methods of ethnicity.

Singers who partake in contemporary voice practice often explore extra-complex sonorities that exceed a single fundamental frequency with gently sloping spectra, such as is normally seen in speech and song. In this recipe, after discussing basic issues of voice, the ingredients of two extra-normal techniques will be presented.

Unlike flute or trumpet, singers are not able to externally manipulate voice. Therefore, the identification of individual parameters that a vocalist uses is not a trivial issue. Even though the number of elements involved in sound production is enormous, an acoustic framework consisting of a driving force, source of acoustic disturbance, resonator, and articulation provide the performer with a powerful conceptual tool that can be reliably used in performance.

Embedded within this framework are numerous factors that humans use when singing: air direction; airflow; vocal-fold tension; subglottal pressure; front to back tongue placement; torso tension; glottal valving; nasality; laryngeal height; sensation of placement of sound; respiratory support, etc.

Research has shown that the production of an aesthetically-pleasing tone by instruments and voices is the result of keeping parameters within certain ratios. However, when parameters are shifted to non-idiomatic ratios, transitions to other sounds may occur; for example, by shifting vocal fold tension from an extremely lax glottis to a hyperpressed glottis in order to produce extra-complex sonorities. These transitions to other, extra-normal sounds are central for some composers and performers.

Some common extended techniques include *Sprechgesang*, reinforced-harmonic singing, subharmonics, registral shift, vocal fry, creaky voice, growl, ingressive phonation (inward airflow vs. outward airflow), and screaming. However, there are other extra-normal techniques that have not been explored fully. One such category involves multiphonics produced by combining multiple sound sources. Depending on the artistic context, multiple sound sources may occur at any level of the vocal tract. One conceptual framework involves combining voiced and unvoiced sounds in various combinations, such as:

1. Voiced and voiced, such as glottal pitch + ventricular folds (imitated-Tibetan Chant)
2. Voiced and unvoiced, such as glottal pitch + lip buzz
3. Unvoiced and unvoiced, such as pharyngeal articulation + lip buzz

A second and equally powerful framework combines elements within the categories of power, source, resonance, and articulation. For example, one combination involves a nasal air frication with a lingua-dental air frication (power and power); while another combines voice with sustained tongue frication (source and articulation).

The sounds that seem hardest to quantify are those numerous methods for producing voiced multiphonics (voiced & voiced). There has been very little systematic research done in this area, though some performers, such as Phil Minton, have explored such methods. Figure 1 presents a fully voiced biphonic sonority that seems to involve two separate modes in the male voice; a low tone that is more or less stable combined with a whistle tone. The steps to producing this biphonic sound may include: 1.) producing ordinary voice, 2.) shift ordinary tone to nasal cavity, 3.) tighten the front part of the vocal folds, 4.) sing the so-called creaky voice (sing lowest tone, then go lower) keeping the vocal folds lax, 5.) widen lips and jaw mouth, 6.) imagine, then allow higher transient pitches (whistles) to be sustained.

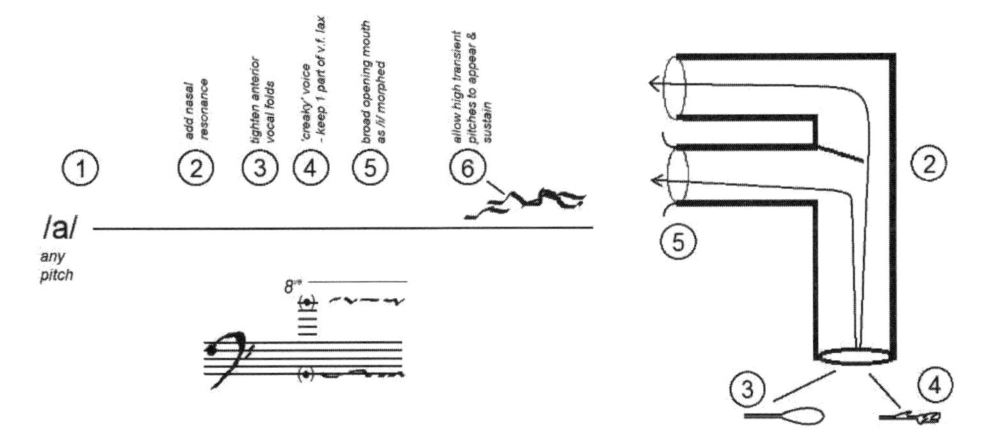


Figure 1: One procedure for producing a fully voiced biphonic sound that seems to involve two simultaneous modes of vibration. The sound involves a low, stable nasal tone that is combined with a higher tone in the whistle register (M3)

A second voiced multiphonic involves the glottal whistle that occurs at the superior boundary of the glottis that feels and sounds like a whistle produced in the throat. Figure 2 outlines a few tendencies for finding this. 1.) Using ingressive or egressive airflow, search for a high resonant tone by raising the palate, 2.) using low airflow, 3.) using either a lax glottis or alternatively a tightly constricted glottis with high subglottal air pressure, 4.) no oscillation of the vocal folds, 5. & 6.) using lower torso and abdominal tension while relaxing upper torso and neck, 7.) try a nasal placement.

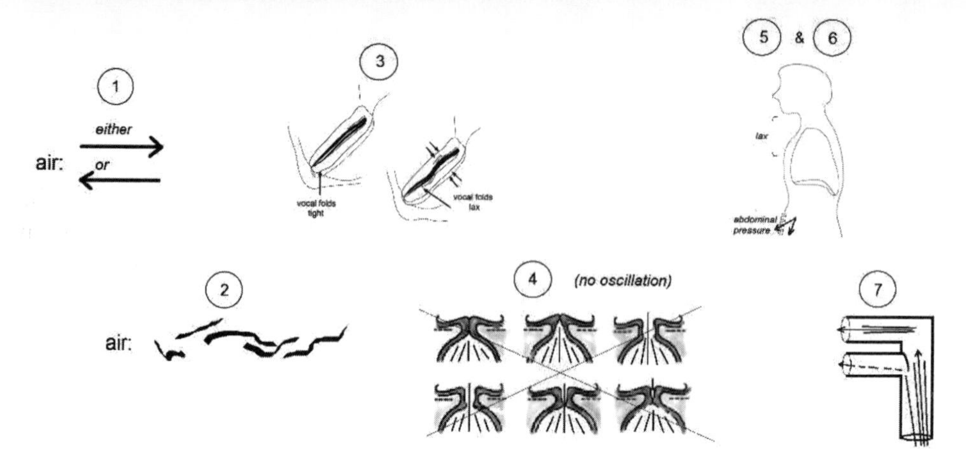


Figure 2: One potential procedure to produce the glottal whistle (M4) using either an ingressive or egressive airflow.

**Read More About It:**

https://michaeledwardedgerton.wordpress.com/compositional-catalogue-by-ensemble/

RECIPE

# Icing the Song: Onsets and Releases in Rock Singing

*Matthew Edwards*

There are many technical differences between rock and classical singing. Among the easiest to address are onsets and releases. Onsets and releases are like the icing on a cake. The cake itself must be good, but the icing and decorations are usually what make it pop. In rock singing, if the onsets and releases are too clean, it is like eating a cake with no icing.

**INGREDIENTS:**
Clean
Aspirate
Glottal
Fry
Growl
Scoops
Fall-offs

**SERVES:**
Established and aspiring rock singers who are ready to begin polishing their songs.

In a clean/simultaneous onset, the vocal folds begin vibrating at the same time air is released. In a clean release, the airflow and vocal fold vibration stop simultaneously. This type of onset/release is most often found in classical and musical theatre styles. The /u/ and /o/ vowels on a simple pattern are usually quite effective in eliciting a clean onset in students who are struggling to find the quality.

Aspirate onsets are common in pop music and rock ballads. In an aspirate onset, the singer exhales before allowing the vocal folds to come together in vibration. It is as if there is an invisible /h/ before the word. Aspirate releases are the reverse; the vocal folds fall apart as air continues to release. If a student is struggling to find this quality, have him sing, "I love you" on a 5–4–3–2–1 pattern as if he is two inches from a lover's ear. Instruct him to feel as if he is on the verge of whispering.

In a glottal onset, the vocal folds come together firmly and are held for a millisecond before being set into motion by the breath. This creates a "pop" at the beginning of phonation. A glottal release is similar, but in this case the singer abruptly closes the vocal folds, which stops airflow and vibration at the same time. If a student is struggling to create a glottal onset, have him hold his breath and then sing. For glottal releases, ask him to suddenly hold his breath at the end of the phrase and add a slight "uh" at the end if desired.

I like using the phrase "I gotta get outta here" on a single pitch with a driving rhythm in the accompaniment to teach this quality.

Fry onsets are common in many styles and are a result of the vocal folds vibrating sporadically. To create a fry onset, the vocal folds touch lightly together and are set into vibration by the breath. When this happens, the vibration is aperiodic and there is no discernable pitch. After a few milliseconds, the vocal folds fall into a regular vibration cycle and settle on an exact pitch. In a fry release, the vocal folds begin on pitch, but the intrinsic muscles slightly release from their adducted position, allowing the vocal folds to vibrate sporadically. Some students will make the fry by forcing their vocal folds together; this approach will quickly tire them out. Instead, help your students find vocal fry by carrying head voice down into the lowest part of their range until the vocal folds begin to flap around. This quality should have a lot of airflow. When a student has mastered bringing the top down, teach her to initiate in that position. When she can initiate a healthy fry without bringing head voice down, begin gliding up and down in the lower part of her range with fry quality. Then try to glide up into a specific pitch. This should help her learn how to apply fry to the beginning of phrases.

Growls are a more aggressive form of intentional vocal distortion and the mechanics are not yet fully understood. It is likely the sound is produced in a variety of ways including pharyngeal constriction that brings the false vocal folds together, pharyngeal wall vibration caused by intense airflow, and/or vibration of the tissues in the back of the mouth including the uvula and tonsils. Regardless of how it is produced, it is a harsh vocal quality that requires a great deal of practice to produce in a safe manner. If a student already knows how to create this sound and is not feeling discomfort, you should feel comfortable allowing him to continue to do so. If he does not know how to produce this quality, and you are not comfortable teaching it, it is probably best to refer him to someone who specializes in extended techniques. These sounds can be produced in a relatively healthy manner with proper instruction.

Scoops occur at the onset and are pretty self-explanatory—the singer scoops into the note. Some scoops are quick, others are more of a slide. Some begin on an exact pitch while others begin randomly. Fall-offs are the release version of the scoop. In a fall-off, the final pitch of a vocal line falls as the note is released. In some styles, the final note is exact. However, it is more common for the final note to be random and frequently the pitch is indiscernible.

It is important to note that all of these should be performed with the minimum effort necessary to accomplish the desired quality. Rock singers always perform on microphone and should allow the amplification to do the work. Many sounds that rock singers make may sound aggressive, but can be produced in a healthy manner with a microphone a few millimeters away from the lips. Since the singer does not need to worry about acoustic amplitude, he can take smaller breaths and use less breath pressure when singing. This will help alleviate excess pressure that could lead to vocal fatigue and/or damage.

There are two ways to use this information in your teaching. If you are working with an established commercial singer, simply being aware of the wide variety of acceptable onsets and releases is a step in the right direction. If you notice that the student is using the same choices over and over again, bring it up and ask if she is interested in adding some variety to her work. If you are working with a singer who is new to commercial styles, integrate these onsets and releases into her technical exercises. For example, use word phrases (i.e., "help me get away") on simple tonal patterns in the lower part of the student's range. For men, I usually begin with a 1–3–5–3–1 pattern starting on E3 in chest register; for women, I start around B3 in chest or chest-mix. Spend several minutes trying each of the onsets and releases one at a time. Then have the student sing the same phrase using one type of onset and a different type of release. Talk to her about how those changes affect the music. After you have introduced her to the concept, assign several songs for her to analyze for the following lesson. Ask her to practice imitating every onset and release she hears on the recordings. When she can successfully copy the original artist, ask her to bring the same song the following week but with her own choices for onsets and releases. With a little practice, she will be icing her songs like Martha Stewart ices a cake.

RECIPE

# Vocal Animal Crackers

*Robert Edwin*

Animal kingdom "voices" are acoustic instruments capable of an almost unlimited variety of sounds. Many acoustic instruments, however, have fixed resonators. The wooden body of a stringed instrument, the tubing of brass, the casing of a drum, all have defined shapes that produce limited resonance choices from the sound source; namely the strings, mouthpiece, and drumstick. Because we humans (and other animals) have flexible resonators—the throat, mouth, and nose—we can change the shape of those resonators, thus changing the tonal quality from our sound source: the vocal folds ("cords") located in the larynx ("voice box"). For vocal health and flexibility as well as increased repertoire choices, it is pedagogically advantageous for teachers to encourage their student singers of all ages to explore vocal animal crackers and discover all the sounds they can create.

**INGREDIENTS:**

One imaginary animal crackers box filled with a wide variety of creatures from aardvarks to zebras.

A teacher ready, willing, and able to take singing students on an expansive vocal journey.

Singers willing to take that journey with their minds and voices.

A random selection of musical patterns, including scales and arpeggios; as well as myriad sounds such as grunts, groans, and squeals that exist in the animal kingdom.

**SERVES:**

A singer's vocal technique by expanding tonal options and exercising the total singing system from top to bottom; cross-training opportunities to give singers the potential to sing in a variety of genres; creative stimulation for both teacher and student.

**The Recipe:**

Since real animal cracker boxes contain a limited and often unidentifiable number of fauna, the imaginary animal cracker box will prove much more pedagogically flexible and beneficial. In this recipe, both student and teacher can choose the animals.

To get started, tell the student, "Here is my imaginary box of animal crackers filled with every creature you can think of. Reach into the box and pick out an animal whose sound you'd like to imitate." If a lion is chosen, a musical "roar" would be in order. Encourage the student to act out the sound to reinforce the singer-actor connection in voice technique as well as repertoire. However, caution the student to avoid overly violent and excessive sounds that could potentially damage the vocal mechanism. Repeat this exercise letting the student choose a variety of animals to imitate. If students can't think of any creatures, provide one from your pre-thought-out list.

Teachers can be task-specific by choosing animals whose sounds address a specific vocal issue. For example, a student who has a consistently nasal tone quality in singing can be asked to imitate an animal sound that requires lifting the soft palate into its closed position. Cows and their "moo" and large dogs with their "woofs" work well. To make the exercise more musical, use a triad or a five-note diatonic scale as the pattern for the sound. Conversely, if a student's default tonality sounds like "Rocky" in the movies and Broadway show of the same name, lowering the soft palate with animal sounds such as the "quack" of a duck or the "baaaa" of a sheep can access more treble-dominant tonal options.

Students who only sing in one-register can be encouraged to explore their other register via selective animal sounds. For example, a boy or man who has an unused Mode 2 ("head voice") register, can stimulate that muscle via the "hoo" of the owl or the "tweet" of the canary. On the other hand, a girl or woman who rarely or never uses the Mode 1 ("chest voice") register might benefit from a guard dog's "arf, arf, arf" on pitches below or around middle C (C4). Register transitions can be addressed by expanding the musical intervals in the exercises. For example, a donkey's "hee haw" with a Mode 2 "hee" and a Mode 1 "haw" an octave apart can engage both registers as well as work on the mix by blending and balancing the sounds. Wolves and their elongated "ahroos" and cats with their "meows" are other useful options.

"Vocal animal crackers" can be a challenging exercise and may be too intimidating for new or beginning students. The teacher must be able to assess the student's comfort level and risk-taking potential before incorporating this unusual "dish" into a lesson.

The ingredients in this recipe are practically endless, limited only by imagination and creativity. For almost every vocalization possible, there is an animal sound ready to serve teacher and student. Bark on!

RECIPE

# The Changing Boy's Voice: From Rocky Road to Sublime Smoothie

*Patrick K. Freer*

Working through the challenges of the changing voice is difficult for teachers. Imagine being the boy! Many boys who sing consistently through childhood into adolescence have developed muscular conditioning that facilitates easy singing during the voice change. Other boys, particularly those who lack a foundation of good singing technique, will experience significant discomfort and frustration when trying to sing during the process of adolescent vocal development. The good news is that there is something choral music teachers can do to help!

Research with boys around the world suggests that adolescent boys who withdraw from singing would have stayed involved if they felt confident about why their voice was changing, how it would change, what they could do to continue singing, and how to use vocal technique to maximize their new-found vocal capabilities.[1] That's our job as voice and choral music teachers . . . to provide foundational vocal instruction for boys with "Rocky Road" voices so that they can sing whenever and wherever they wish. What about the "Sublime Smoothie" part of the recipe? One of Atlanta's most famous foodie shops is Sublime Doughnuts. I conducted a boy's ensemble in Atlanta a few months ago. I used the analogy of "singing is like a smoothie" and I asked what would make the smoothie better. One boy said, "Mixing in a Sublime Doughnut so that it becomes a Sublime Smoothie." The boys decided the analogy worked well: Many voices move from "Rocky Road" to "Smoothie" but they need to mix in "Sublime" vocal technique along the way. That's what we'll explore in the following recipe.

**INGREDIENTS:**
Adolescent Boys
Adolescent Boys' Voices
Teacher's Healthy Vocal Model
Teacher's Solid Vocal Knowledge
Patience
A 12-year-old's Sense of Humor

**SERVES:**
Boys aged 10 to 15; their peer students; their parents; the choir; the community of choral singing; your soul.

1 For example, see Patrick K. Freer, "Perspectives of European Boys about their Voice Change and School Choral Singing: Developing the Possible Selves of Adolescent Male Singers," *British Journal of Music Education* 32, no. 1, (2015): 87–106.

Start with the basic ingredients of singing technique. These include bodily relaxation, proper physical alignment, a coordinated breath management system, the process of beginning to phonate on a pitch, and how to transform all of that into a sung musical exercise or phrase. These ingredients work with all voices including adolescent boys, however those boys who are not familiar or confident with the ingredients need extra attention from their teachers before they get frustrated and burn out. Even with the proper ingredients, good technique is necessary for students to know how to combine those ingredients into a satisfying singing experience.

Teachers, like good chefs, need to identify when something is missing and figure out what needs to be added in order to achieve the desired effect. When working with adolescent boys, two things are often at play. Some boys know the different elements of singing (the "rocks" in "rocky road"), but don't know how to coordinate them into a smooth process ("smoothie"). Whereas a second group of boys will not know the basic elements of singing. For them, these elements are all new, and the production of smooth and coordinated singing can be frustratingly elusive.

Choral teachers should use the warm-up session to teach, directly, the elements of vocal technique. Then, those elements can be practiced in the repertoire rehearsal segments that follow. Teachers should consider their job as teaching voice skills in a group setting, with repertoire specifically chosen to allow practice with those newly-acquired or newly-honed skills.

Boys with changing voices often have difficulty "putting it all together." Eliminate what you can so that boys can focus on what is most important by breaking down the "recipe" of smooth singing into its individual ingredients. For instance, it may not be of utmost importance that a boy can sing a particular phrase if he is having difficulty phonating on any of the pitches in the first place. Begin with where the boy is comfortable singing, even if it is on a pitch not found in the repertoire. Gain his trust and build his confidence by helping him sing comfortably and smoothly in his preferred pitch range, and then gradually apply those same technical skills as you lead him to sing in other parts of his range. Help him understand how he can control his air flow/speed by using his abdominal musculature, help him build toward a smooth flow of exhaled air with a smooth contraction of that musculature, and then help him learn to sustain a pitch with that smooth flow of air. Many boys will experience success once they understand the basic technical elements of singing . . . elements that remain the same during each stage of the boy's voice-change process.[2]

And, if you're unfamiliar with the techniques of singing, do what you would do if you wanted to learn a new cooking technique . . . take lessons. Don't be afraid to take a voice lesson or two so that you can be the most effective singing teacher for your students. That would be sublime!

2 Patrick K. Freer, *The Young Adolescent Voice. Getting Started with Middle School Choir*, 2nd ed. (Lanham, MD: Rowman & Littlefield Education, 2009), 61–76.

RECIPE

# Transitioning from Dinner to Dessert: *Passaggio* in Contemporary Singing

*J.D. Frizzell*

Contemporary styles like pop, jazz, and musical theatre often require a different sound than is used in classical styles. In addition to more relaxed vowel shapes, more glissandi, and less vibrato, these styles often require a unified tone throughout the range—basically the removal of *passaggio* (transition area between vocal registers). Combined with the increased use of chest voice, this means that a singer's range becomes much more limited in contemporary styles. Many choral directors and musical theatre singers refer to "chest voice" and "mixed voice" when describing ways to increase the usable range in contemporary styles. However, these terms are limited in physiological accuracy. By exploring various laryngeal positions and vocal fold muscle usage, we can provide more useful tools for contemporary singing.

**INGREDIENTS:**
Laryngeal positions
Jaw shapes
Resonating cavities
Vocal folds
Patience
An open mind

**SERVES:**
Pop, jazz, and musical theatre songs; an even tone throughout the range.

Throughout a decade of teaching and developing contemporary singing within the context of a traditional choral program, I explored various methods of helping singers achieve a healthy singing tone, regardless of musical style. Early on, I discovered that while students explored their voices, ignoring the terms chest voice and head voice was helpful in removing artificial barriers. This is a main component of "Spectrum Singing," a system for singing in all styles, developed by Dr. Erin Hackel. Truly revolutionary, this method opened up an entirely new world of possibilities for my students. Her terms and categorizations codified a lot of the techniques I was already using with some success. This recipe is built upon my work with "Spectrum Singing."

Successful singing in almost all styles involves the coordination of two vocal fold muscle sets, the thryoarytenoids (TAs) and the cricothyroids (CTs). For untrained or inexperienced singers, the TAs, also known as the true vocal folds, are a larger set of muscles almost always used, while the CTs are a smaller set of muscles utilized less often and with less understanding. For our recipe, we simply need to understand that these muscles exist and play an important coordinating role with each other. "Spectrum Singing" identifies four "gears," each of which involve a different combination of TA and CT function:

- Neutral (fourth gear): all CT. Used in falsetto in men and head voice in women.
- Slope (third gear): mostly CT, 1/4 of TA. Used by many jazz and musical theatre singers. Normal speaking voice larynx position.
- Incline (second gear): half CT, half TA. Used by pop and contemporary musical theatre singers. Higher laryngeal position.
- Full (first gear): all TA. Used by male operatic singers and female singers in their low range. Low laryngeal position.[1]

Many singers, especially younger or untrained, tend to either exclusively use neutral or full. They often need encouragement and training to explore their voices in a way that will allow them to discover slope and incline, which are necessary for healthy contemporary singing.

**Mixing the Ingredients:**
Start by introducing them to the various gears and have them listen to an example of each gear performed by famous singers; YouTube is a great resource. Examples include:

- Neutral: Most children's and girl choirs, boy sopranos, male falsettists/countertenors, most classical female singers
- Slope: Ella Fitzgerald, Julie Andrews, Gertrude Lawrence, New York Voices, The Real Group
- Incline: Adam Lambert, Idina Menzel, Tori Kelly, Kristin Chenoweth, Bruno Mars, Katy Perry
- Full: Luciano Pavarotti, Jose Carreras, most teenage female voices trying to "belt"

Once students understand the gears conceptually, they can practice laryngeal position independently. Have the singers put their finger on their larynx and try to move it up and down without phonating. Once they can maneuver the larynx, add a single pitch in a comfortable range and then move the position around.

Next, use the Spectrum warm-up, which begins with a neutral, far "back" placement on a closed vowel sound [u]. Placing your hand beside your head as a physical representation of placement, begin to move the sound more "forward" or "bright" and shift gradually to a more open vowel sound [ɛ], [ə], or [i].

Singers will need extensive practice combining the tonal placement with laryngeal position before they are able to fully control their TA and CT function, thereby switching between these gears. Once they can do so, use the gears often in a voice lesson or rehearsal. You can use the term "gear switch" to illustrate a stylistic demand of a particular song, or instruct students to "change to 4" or "change to 2" as a way just to practice the various gears. Spending the time to teach students how to adjust in these ways can lead them to incredible breakthroughs in singing contemporary music without fear of their "break."

1 For more information see, Erin Hackel, "Teaching Your Singers to Sing in All Styles," in *A Cappella Warm-Ups for Pop and Jazz Choirs*, eds. Deke Sharon and J.D. Frizzell, (Milwaukee: Hal Leonard Publishing, 2017), 15–23.

RECIPE

# Cookin' with Gas: Breathing Facts, Best Practices, and Helpful Imagery

*Jeannie Gagné*

Breathing is one of the voice lesson topics that sends singers into fits of anxiety and self-doubt. "I don't know how to breathe!" they say. (Yes, you do, you're quite alive). Students are confused by breathing instruction into areas of the body that don't actually contain air, such as the belly or pelvic floor. With all best intentions, teachers use various images to help students take in sufficient air and manage its release and pressure, while keeping neck-area muscles as free as possible. But often what one teacher says is the *right* way to breathe, another says is *wrong*. No wonder students are confused and tense!

A good practice for solving this confusion is to lay out anatomical facts along with imagery and physical practice. When students correctly understand how their body works, they will learn how to more easily be both relaxed and actively supported when they sing. They will learn how to release the muscles not needed, while engaging those that are necessary.

**INGREDIENTS:**

Inhalation: Use slow, deep breaths as needed and when possible
Exhalation: Stir slowly when blending with legato tones, increase pressure for strong-tone breath support
Regular exercise: This component is a must in every recipe for a full-bodied, tasty result.
Anatomical awareness of the vocal process: Knowing how your stove works enables you to cook like a pro!

**SERVES:**

Improved tone and flexibility, personal growth, together with overall body-mind wellness.

New science shows us that the best way to change a learned movement is by altering your approach to it, instead of trying to stop doing it. For example, is the student breathing too high and shallow into the chest? To shift this, focus the student's attention elsewhere, such as on their feet or midsection. Don't even mention the upper chest. Say something like, "breathe as if you are filling a donut float around your midsection." Don't say, "*don't* breathe high in your chest!" That's because when you try *not* to do something, you still reinforce that movement simply by giving it your attention, whether positive or negative. But when you practice a new approach, and stop thinking about what you're doing wrong, you can teach your body the new skill. With repetition, the new approach becomes habit and the old one dissolves away.

Here are some concepts that are particularly effective for healthy, effective breath management:

- Singing is a wind instrument. Air pressure comes up from the lungs to bring the vocal folds together in vibration. Controlling the release of air in conjunction with true vocal fold vibration is how we can sing loudly without strain, for example, or sing high and softly with a controlled vibrato. The way air pressure brings the folds together is an example of the *Bernoulli Effect*.
- When we are tense, muscles tighten and restrict movement throughout the body; knees lock and shoulders constrict. If a student fears being "wrong"—especially when standing in front of a teacher who "sees all, knows all, hears all"—they will be *really* tight. Encouraging full-body movements during vocalizing releases this tension and frees the breath.
- The word breath "control" causes students to think they are supposed to somehow constrict breathing muscles, often resulting in tension. Use terms like "breath management" and "breath support" instead.
- Where and what *is* the diaphragm anyway? Students don't know! It's a large dome-shaped muscle, connected all the way around the torso to the base of the ribs and anchored at the lumbar spine. It separates the torso in half: lungs and heart above, everything else below.
- The diaphragm *always* contracts downward with every breath you take, throughout your life. (We don't actually pull air into our lungs; instead, when the chest cavity is enlarged, a vacuum space is created and air rushes in to fill it.) On exhalation the diaphragm relaxes, pushing air back out again. Therefore, you *always* "breathe from your diaphragm" in a sense, though the diaphragm does not fill with air, since it's a muscle and not a lung. Your ribs also rise and expand when you inhale, and relax when you exhale.
- Your body is quite flexible when it comes to breathing. High or low, shallow or deep, the body likes to breathe to stay alive. When you sing you aren't in danger of drowning. Over-fixating on breathing can engage the sympathetic "fight, flight, or flee" nervous system, or "freak out!"
- "Belly breaths" are relaxing and better for the neck and shoulders, but don't engage the core abdominal muscles that help control the release of air up through the larynx. (You can't breathe into your belly anyway, it has guts, not air! The diaphragm pushes down on belly organs with each inhalation, making your stomach push out.)
- Your upper abdominal muscles have a relationship with your diaphragm. Breaths focused around the lower ribs help expand the base of the lungs where they are larger. Then, engaging the upper abdominal muscles lightly *after* inhalation helps to slow down the rate of exhalation. It feels a bit like gently holding your breath as you release a small stream of air.
- Exercise gets your body into the habit of breathing more deeply. Sit-ups are good for developing upper abdominal tone, as long as you don't do sit ups like crunches that tug on your neck.
- "Spend" less air in the beginning of a phrase when you have more, and budget some to sing the end of the phrase, too.
- When we speak, we tend to inhale at the last moment, after a natural *apnea* or pause at the end of each exhalation. For singing, whenever you have time in the music, inhale more slowly. This has many benefits:
  - Breathing in more slowly encourages a deep breath, and helps the laryngeal muscles from over-tensing.

- Slow breaths prevent "fight, flight, or flee" mode by engaging the calming side of your nervous system.
- While inhaling slowly, picture the note and place it before you phonate.

Though these are but a few examples, this recipe has been tested in many vocal kitchens and works well. The result is an overall goal of demystifying the practice of breathing for singing. The more we de-stress our students, the better you both feel and the better they sing. Also, experiment with adding other ingredients during the lesson, like movement to encourage lower-body breaths such as opening arms, bending knees for high notes, and putting awareness into the feet for grounding. Serve hot, and enjoy!

RECIPE

# Cooking Up Popular Styles and a Healthy Belt Voice

*Kelly K. Garner*

Cooking up popular styles with a healthy "belt voice" can create a "fire in the kitchen" due to the challenges belting presents. Belting should be used and performed in a healthy way, which will enable the popular singer to sing with another "gear" of vocal power and expression within the wildly competitive marketplace of commercial singing.

**INGREDIENTS:**
Jaw jutting
Mask placement
Vowel modification

**SERVES:**
Popular style belters.

One of the most common mistakes that "belters" display when trying to sing convincingly in popular styles is "jaw jutting", that is, an extended jaw position that they feel will enable them to achieve a stylistic effect. Instead, singers should have a relaxed jaw position with a forward and high, "smiling" singing placement in the mask area of the face, combined with open spacing in the back of the throat, enabling the soft palate to arch and the tongue to relax and lower. Many times, singers think they have to do something additional with the jaw in order to sing. The truth of the matter is, the more they can relax and use less tension, the easier their singing will become.

To get the singer to release the jaw, it is sometimes useful to get them to hold the jaw back with a finger on the cleft of the chin, or the teacher might also take the singers's jaw in their hand and wiggle it back and forth as the vocalist tries to sing. This interaction enables them to understand that they do not need to tighten the jaw to project while singing. Prior to applying this strategy, it is important to determine if the vocalist has experienced any symptoms of Temporo-Mandibular Joint Syndrome, often referred to as TMJ. If the singer has experienced any such issue with TMJ, teachers need to be careful with putting any kind of pressure on the singer's jaw as they are singing, in order to not pop the jaw out of joint or aggravate the TMJ in any way.

Once the jaw is somewhat released, and sometimes even before it releases completely, have singers also try the following technique. Instruct singers to speak the lyric with an accent as if they were from Fargo, North Dakota (Far GOH, North Da KOH tah). This is usually referred to as vowel modification. Modifying vowels slightly in this way will create more space in the mouth and back of the throat. Feel free to use other analogies of speaking as if singers were from Minnesota (Min-ne SOH ta) or even New York (New YAHK). Then have them speak the phrase they are trying to belt in a spoken kind of way. Some teachers call this "shout style" but instead of having them "shout," so to speak, have them speak the phrase as if they're wanting to get someone's attention from across the room. Next, have singers echo the phrase over and over, repeating after you model, and raise the pitch (even though we are only speaking) of the "belted" note on each repetition until the desired pitch that they are belting in the song is reached.

This is a technique that over the years I have seen work to somewhat "trick" the singer into realizing the belted voice, or particular note in popular styles and sounds, they are trying to achieve need not be as difficult and tight as they believe is necessary in order to be effective. Truly relaxed and healthy belting for popular styles is more about being completely relaxed and using the breath support to suspend the breath and maintain a constant stream of air. Many popular style singers hurt themselves by using too much tension in trying to "belt." In order for the popular singer to "belt" healthily, they must use this technique and strategy in order to release ANY jaw tension.

Relaxing the tongue is also a big part of belting healthily. If the tongue is tight, it will only pull up and stretch the vocal tract, which causes unwanted tension and will also make the acoustic space much smaller in the back of the throat. This small space in the back of the throat, that some immature "belter's" try to create, will not only make singing feel more difficult, but will also cause the vocal tone to sound very small and uncomfortably bright.

The goal for the belted sound in popular style singing always is for it to be warm, round and full. Singing in a popular style as it relates to belting is simply the journey of getting the singer to realize that they are working too hard. If singers can get to the point of complete freedom and relaxation, then the mechanism components (the jaw, the tongue, vocal tract, etc.) will also relax and the singer will not be able to believe how much easier singing and "belting" in a popular style can really be.

So, take a chill pill in the vocal "kitchen!" Get out of the frying pan and RELAX!

RECIPE

# Cross Training Ingredients for the Female Belt and Classical Voice

*Kathryn Green*

Today's singers are expected to sing in a broad spectrum of styles. A singer greatly augments their capacity for employment if they are able to cross train and sing in both classical and contemporary commercial music (CCM) styles. This recipe covers a female producing a musical theatre belt voice and a classical voice quality. For a singer to be able to produce both of these qualities at an elite level, there are a number of elements that need to be adjusted for each voice quality.

**INGREDIENTS:**
Vibrato
Articulation & Phrasing
Breath Support
Registration Negotiation
Pharyngeal Space

**SERVES:**
Singers and Teachers.

**Cross Training Recipe:**

1. **Vibrato**
   - **Classical Ingredient: Consistent, even vibrato from the onset**. This is one of the hallmarks of a good classical singer. Starting any phrase with a straight tone is not appropriate in most classical repertoire.
   - **Belt Ingredient: Straight tone onset that moves to a vibrato**. Broadway agents and casting directors often mention the vibrato in a voice as being too classical. It may be one of the most telling signs of a classically trained singer and can cause more than a few failed auditions in the musical theatre world.
2. **Articulation & Phrasing**
   - **Classical Ingredient: Precise pronunciation and legato line.** Plosive, crisp consonants that interject between vowels at a 1% to 99% ratio of consonant to vowel. This produces a legato line and clearly enunciated words.
   - **Belt Ingredient: Speech-like pronunciation.** Sing like you speak, which translates to text-driven phrasing that gives equal time to vowels and consonants. Although the text is of paramount importance in musical theatre, colloquial pronunciation is preferred over a precisely enunciated approach.

3. **Breath Support**
   Breath Support has long been established since the inception of voice training as one of the most critical elements in producing a beautiful timbre. The question is how important is it in the belted voice? Moreover, perhaps an even more important question would be, is the objective of a successful belt to produce a beautiful sound? Power and dramatic intensity might be more in line with the objectives of a belter. However, it would be right to say that both qualities require support from the airflow generated by the lungs.
   - **Classical Ingredient: *Appoggio!* Breath support is essential to the classical voice.** The female classical voice will generally not have as great a closed quotient as the belted voice. In other words, the vocal folds will allow more air through the passageway than the belted. This difference makes it more critical for the classical female singer to have a substantial breath intake and ability to manage the outflow of that breath, at the vocal fold level, in order to maintain a resonant tone and complete each phrase.
   - **Belt Ingredient: Breath, but not as much or as low and deep.** The belted voice has a higher closed quotient than a classical production. This translates into the vocal folds literally not allowing the breath to flow through as easily. Therefore, less breath is required in a belt as the vocal folds stop it from escaping, which builds subglottal pressure that gives the sound even more brilliance. It is also true that an inhalation that does not involve a low breath intake, avoids the tracheal pull, which lowers the laryngeal position and can cause more constriction when pulling up a chest production at a high volume.
4. **Registration Negotiation**
   Register negotiation is always a matter of balancing the two qualities produced by the ratio of cricothyroid to thyroarytenoid muscular antagonism. Any good voice production is going to have a mix of both of these qualities; otherwise we would be hearing a bellow or a breathy falsetto.
   - **Classical Ingredient: Head or "Whoop" dominant.** The classical female voice is primarily head dominant.
   - **Belt Ingredient: "Call" or Chest dominant.** However, well-produced belt voice probably has much more head quality in it then one would suspect despite the fact that it is by nature more chest-dominant.
5. **Pharyngeal space**
   The shape of the throat can dramatically alter the vocal quality.
   - **Classical Ingredient: Big pharyngeal space.** Voice teachers have long been advising their classical students to produce "long, tall" vowels. Another admonition is to sing with an "open" throat. Classical singing often involves:
     a. raising the soft palate.
     b. lowering the larynx upon inhalation.
     c. elongating the pharynx by "pooching" the lips forward.
   - **Belt Ingredient: Shortened pharyngeal space.** It is a fact: the belted voice causes the larynx to raise. A singer does not purposely work to raise it, but it raises of its own accord. Other aspects of minimizing the space are:
     a. Allowing the soft palate to remain in a "speech-like" position.
     b. Lips in a lateral position, avoiding closed vowel shapes [u] in order to produce a high belt sound free of constriction.
     c. A slight tilt of the chin upward on the highest notes which allows the larynx to raise.

You can begin to successfully negotiate CCM and classical repertoire with these simple tools. A great resource for further study is *The Vocal Athlete* by Marci Rosenberg and Wendy LeBorgne. Enjoy!

RECIPE

# Movement: Finding the Perfect Seasonings for each Recipe

*Erin Hackel*

For many singers, there is a "curtain of doubt" pulled over the idea of expressing a piece of music through movement. The idea that there's only one *correct* way of using one's body through space, or that there are certain rules that must be assiduously learned and applied, as one does with diction or baroque ornamentation. Self-conscious gestures, nervous hand movements, and over-thinking can make any beautifully prepared vocal piece uncomfortable for performer and audience alike. Luckily, this "curtain of doubt" is quickly swept aside with some carefully applied ideas. In fact, with time and thought, every singer will be able to collect several completely individual spice mixtures that they can customize for each song, seasoning each one perfectly, and differently, for every performance.

**INGREDIENTS:**
1 Well-prepared song in any genre
1 Curious mind; any age or experience will do
A dash of bravery

**SERVES:**
All singers and teachers of singing.

Have students prepare each song according to their recipe. Depending on genre, this will involve several separate techniques. All songs should be cooked until well-done. Once perfectly prepared, you are ready to season.

Help students go through the following steps:

**Step One:**
Know that you, your body, and your mind have been training to be expressive since you were a baby. You have been learning how to portray your needs, emotions and thoughts for years and years. You're already very good at this, an expert, even. Even better, you know best how to move your own body through space. It's not how others move; how could it be? Your arms are your own, your legs, how you move your head when you are listening, how you use your hands when you are excited. The biggest mistake singers make in this step is to try to imitate how someone else's body moves. You haven't been practicing those for years, and you probably aren't very good at them. *Remember, you're the expert at moving your body in life, and in singing.*

**Step Two:**
Approach your finished song and examine it carefully. You must know, in broad strokes, the overall emotional arc of the song. How does this emotion affect your own body? Allow this to steep for quite a bit; feel this emotion as genuinely as you can and see how it makes you stand, and how the set of your shoulders and expression on your face changes. *This is where you begin the song, with this posture that is uniquely your own expression of that emotion, not an imitation of another's.*

**Step Three:**
You've broadly seasoned your song, but a wonderful performance requires a few more steps from you. Examine your song more minutely. Allow the lyrics to honestly guide your body. Experiencing emotions will make your body move in genuine ways that are easily relatable to all humans. Have no reservation or fear, this is something you have been doing all your life, you can't do it "wrong." Allow these words to be your own. Doing this requires that last dash of bravery, yes, but you are the only singer who can season this song exactly the way you do. Even older pieces, with very few lyrics, are a wonderful vehicle for your own individual and unique way of moving. Find your own story that matches the broad emotion of the song. Tell it to us in as much detail as you can. *If you tell us a story that you believe in, using the natural expression your body has been practicing for years, you will have created a piece of art.*

A few tips from having prepared this recipe with my students several times:

- An ill-prepared song will yield very poor results.
- Larger, broader movements work best on stage, but the emotional work driving your performance will naturally create everything else you need for success.
- The rests are where you get to tell us even more about how you seasoned the song.
- There is power in well-placed stillness.
- Insincerity is something we are all well trained to dislike. Do not season your song with this spice.
- There is no "correct" movement for any song. Your well-mixed thoughts and honest response to emotions are perfect.
- You do not need to be coordinated, a dancer, or elegant to be excellent at this recipe. See Step Three.

RECIPE

# The Sweet Desserts of Laryngeal Stability Through Refined Vocal Acoustics

*David Harris*

Contemporary voice science has shown that the vocal folds and vocal tract operate on a non-linear source/filter model.[1] This means that what happens in the vocal tract feeds back to the vocal folds, creating opportunities for stability or instability. When acoustic feedback is less than optimal, the "thickening muscle" (thyroarytenoid, or TA) often overworks, creating a coordination that relies heavily on that muscle, rather than on a balanced interaction between all of the laryngeal muscles. This is often experienced as Mode 1 dominance, and can create a pressed tone.

Training vocal acoustics through an understanding of vowel shape as separate from vowel perception can help to develop vocal fold stability.[2] Through this process, vocalists create a sensational relationship to distinct vowel shapes, and encourage the arytenoid muscle groups to play a larger role in general, thereby balancing vocal fold muscle coordination.[3] This recipe focuses primarily on the Formant 1 area, or, "the pitch of the air in the throat," and includes a comment about "twang," a sensation that comes from the epilaryngeal tube that resides just above the vocal folds, between the vocal folds and the pharynx.

*Note that the laryngeal registration language of Mode 1 and Mode 2 correlates somewhat with traditional language of "chest voice" (Mode 1), and "head voice" (Mode 2). The traditional terms also include an acoustic element, hence the change in language.[4]

**INGREDIENTS:**

Vocal fold mass/weight values Mode 1, Mode 2, everything in the middle
Arytenoid adduction (focus)
Vowel shape: F1 Vowel Shape Chains

[u] [ʊ] [o] [ɔ] [a] [æ]
[i] [ɪ] [e] [ɛ] [a] [æ]

Tiny, completely easy sound (Mode 2)
Twang (whine, core)
Crescendo

**SERVES:**

One too many: It works superbly in groups, and makes individuals equally delighted.

1 Ingo R. Titze and Katherine Verdolini Abbott, *Vocology: The Science and Practice of Voice Habilitation* (Iowa City: National Center for Voice & Speech, 2012), 296–297.

2 Ian Howell, "Parsing the Spectral Envelope" (DMA diss, New England Conservatory, 2016): 8–10.

3 Christian T. Herbst and Jan G. Svec, "Adjustment of Glottal Configurations in Singing," *Journal of Singing* 70, no. 3 (2014): 302–303.

4 Kenneth W. Bozeman, *Kinesthetic Voice Pedagogy* (Gahanna, OH: Inside View Press, 2017), 80.

**Instructions:**

Prepare your ingredients:

1. Vocal Fold Mass/Weight:
   Combine the vocal fold modes on a middle note in your range on an [o] vowel shape. Begin loudly, in order to feel Mode 1 (the bulk of the vocal folds in vibration), and then sing as softly/easily as you can on the same note to feel Mode 2 (the vocal ligament managing the sound). Repeat multiple times; note the difference, set aside to cool.
2. Arytenoid Adduction:
   Begin on a middle note in your range making the tiniest, easiest sound you can in Mode 2 on an [u] vowel shape and sustain. Listen for focus and clarity in the sound. If it feels slightly strained, or sounds breathy, begin again, listening for a focused, easy sound.
3. Vowel Shape Chain and Formant 1:
   Understand Formant 1 as "the pitch of the air in your throat," and as separate from the sung pitch. This pitch changes with each vowel shape change. The two vowel shape chains you'll use, [u] [ʊ] [o] [ɔ] [a] [æ] and [i] [ɪ] [e] [ɛ] [a] [æ], move from the lowest "pitch of the air in the throat" to the highest. Note that [u] and [i] have the same pitch and each vowel shape along the chain corresponds to the other chain in sequence.

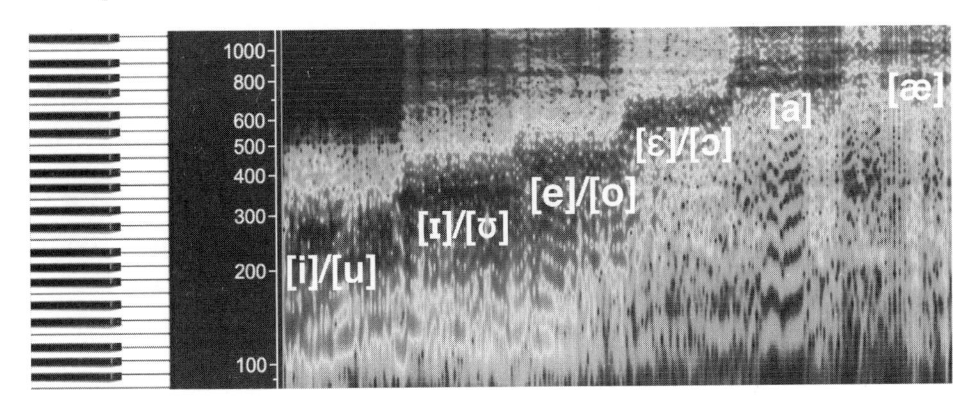


The difference in the vowel perception derives from the "pitch of the air in the mouth" (Formant 2), not shown here. Focusing on the sensational and auditory changes that occur as you change "the pitch of the air in the throat" (Formant 1), sing the vowel chain at medium volume on a single note in the middle of your range. Note that the lower pitched vowel shapes ([u] and [i]) feel more "narrow" than the higher pitched vowel shapes ([a] and [æ]), and that as you sing through the chain, you feel and notice increased "wideness" or "openness."

The dark lines above the IPA in this image from a voice analyzer shows the Formant 1 ("pitch of the air in the throat") values for the vowel shapes in the vowel chains described in this recipe. These shapes represent the full pitch range for the Formant 1 area. Practicing them in this order helps the brain differentiate and fine-tune possible vocal tract adjustments.[5]

5 http://www.voicescienceworks.org/acoustic-registration.html

Mixing Ingredients: Final Preparation

4. Beginning with arytenoid adduction (tiny, easy sound on [u]) sing the vowel chain while maintaining the tiny, easy sound that signifies arytenoid adduction. Importantly, maintain the exact same volume throughout and notice the challenges therein. Repeat and simmer.
5. Once you are comfortable with step 4, begin from the tiny sound on [u], and as you sing through the vowel shape chain, allow your volume to increase so that you end at a loud volume on [ae] in Mode 1. Pay close attention to the volume that corresponds to the middle vowel shapes, as this will relate to the laryngeal "middle ground" between Mode 1 and Mode 2 that is difficult to train, but essential for balanced singing. Pay attention at the loudest moments that you avoid making a pressed sound. One way to help with the transition while avoiding pressure is to tap your hand lightly, guiding the vocal folds to feel "flow." Try this on different sung pitches across your range.

Serve with "whine"

6. Practice whining like a toddler with different vowel shapes. This will help develop epilaryngeal tube focus, otherwise known as "twang," which is a key ingredient in laryngeal stability. You may feel it as "core" to the sound. Once you have a sense of the "whine," sing the vowel shape chain starting on the tiny sound while increasing volume, and let the whine guide the volume increase by feeling like it cores out the sound.

RECIPE

# Ingredients for Good Choral Singing (as opposed to Solo Singing)

*Matthew Hoch*

Adapting one's solo technique to choral situations is something that every singer is called upon to do, yet it remains a perplexing challenge for many. Undergraduate singers—who are usually just beginning to learn the foundations of solo classical technique—often feel pulled in two directions, becoming frustrated as they attempt to give the conductor what he or she wants while simultaneously integrating the technical instruction they are receiving from their applied voice teacher. A solid technique, however, gives the singer the flexibility to sing well and healthily in a variety of styles, and understanding and embracing those stylistic differences is the key to creating a smorgasbord of beautiful choral sounds.

**INGREDIENTS:**
Sensitivity
A flexible voice
Good musicianship
Excellent technique
Respect for one's colleagues
A thorough understanding of style
Keen ears (to sing in tune and match vowels)
Understanding the difference between "choral resonance" and "solo resonance"
Humbleness; putting the ensemble above one's own ego

**SERVES:**
The composer and the music, plain and simple. Good singing is good singing, and much of what is learned in the applied studio carries over beautifully beyond opera and art song to other styles and genres, including choral singing. No choral director in his or her right mind would ever want a choir full of singers who were "less trained," but sometimes well-taught classical singers misunderstand that their role within an ensemble is different than their priorities as a soloist.

Resonance strategy is one key ingredient that must be tweaked in order to achieve a cohesive choral sound. Solo classical singers rely heavily on the "ring" produced by the singer's formant, optimizing vowels in order to project acoustically into the back of the concert hall or opera house. They strive for their voices to be as individually resonant as possible, and a unique timbre is highly desirable. In most choral situations, however, using singer's formant is not desirable. Ensemble singing is about the group—many voices sounding like one—as opposed to drawing attention to the individuality and resonance of one's own voice. Therefore, instead of striving for resonance and "ring," choral singers should listen carefully to those voices around them, matching vowels as carefully as possible, sounding like one within their section, and tuning carefully to the other voice parts. Choral singers should also never sing so loudly that they cannot hear the singers around them. Careful listening and sensitivity is the key.

Misconceptions about vibrato can also be a stumbling block when adapting solo technique to the choral ensemble. Vibrato is muscular resistance to the flow of air. Therefore, since muscles and airflow can be controlled, so can aspects of vibrato. There are two primary components of vibrato: *extent* (degree of pitch variation) and *rate* (number of cycles per second). While rate is more fixed and hardwired within the individual singer, extent is more malleable with practice and training. In most choral situations, a narrower vibrato extent is desirable. What listeners and conductors sometimes perceive as "straight-tone" singing is really just singing with a narrower vibrato extent.

A final point: Many young singers—and too many voice teachers—also do not recognize that solo *Fach* and choral *Fach* are not necessarily the same thing. While a light coloratura soprano might be pleased to sing in the stratosphere for an entire choral concert, a dramatic soprano is likely to become exhausted doing so. Even though she bills herself as a soprano, perhaps singing alto 1 would bring considerable relief and comfort. A heldentenor is also likely to "stick out" on tenor and perhaps he would prefer to sing baritone (bass 1). Lighter voices and lower voice types tend to have less difficulty switching between solo and choral genres. Just like some great athletes are shot putters whereas some are pole vaulters, some singers are more naturally suited to singing Palestrina as opposed to Verdi.

Fortunately, almost every other technical concept taught in the voice lesson—including posture, breath management (*appoggio*), jaw and tongue release, body movement and freedom, and expression—carries over beautifully and with little or no modification when singing in choirs. Other skills, such as study of foreign language study and transcription using the International Phonetic Alphabet (IPA) are invaluable to the choral musician as well. With proper understanding of style, mindful classically trained singers are a key asset to any choral program.

RECIPE

# Putting the 'I' back in Choir: The Delicious Pairing of Individual Voice Instruction in the Choral Rehearsal

*Laurel Irene*

Combining an individual voice teacher and a choral director in the choir rehearsal hasn't always been the most obvious flavor duo. But with a new age of elevating conversations around the voice, crossing aisles and collaborating with colleagues, and voice team models brought forward by the voice medicine world, this combination makes for a complimentary and satisfying meal that draws on everyone's strengths. Most importantly, when instructors unite their offerings at the same table, the singers share in an invaluably amplified experience.

**INGREDIENTS:**
1 choral director
1 individual voice teacher
20–100 choral singers, garnished with individualized instruction
1 heaping scoop of time management
A dash of concise and clear language

**SERVES:**
Millions of vocalist and choral singers across the globe.

**Simple Recipe Combinations:**

*The Choir Retreat*
Choir retreats are a great introductory setting for the individual voice teacher and choral director to share their recipes together. Planning out how you will share the time, down to each 10-minute chunk, is crucial in the planning phase of a retreat. For the individual voice teacher, this can be the time to introduce "know that" information about the voice. This can include images, videos, and concepts that help the singers to "know that" this is what a diaphragm looks like, this is why a silent breath is important, this is what high overtones look like on a voice analyzer, etc. In later rehearsals, the choral director can draw ingredients from this pantry of explanations as she or he is helping the singers to "know how" to integrate those skills into their brain and body habits.

*Integrated Warm-Up*
Having the individual voice teacher lead a vocal warm-up at the beginning of the rehearsal is a great way to share time. A warm-up that serves as the base ingredient for the upcoming

repertoire helps singers build important connections. Discuss vocal challenges of the repertoire, and how the choral director can integrate and apply the concepts covered in the warm-up to the remainder of the rehearsal.

*One-on-One Pull Outs*

Individual needs are difficult to address in a choral rehearsal. The individual voice teacher can be of great service by creating a schedule where each singer is pulled out from rehearsal for a 10 to 15-minute check-in. Voice teachers can explore the following: "When such-and-such vocal instruction is given, how do you interpret it?" and "If such-and-such language used in rehearsal isn't effective for you, how can you translate it for yourself in order to get effective results?" Language that suits each individual in a group is usually impossible to find, but teaching each individual to translate instructions into their own effective language is a goal both the choral director and individual voice teacher can support.

*Sectional Split and Trade*

Split the choir into different rooms so that the individual voice teacher gets to work with half the group while the choral director works with the other half. Swap half way through or during the next sectional so that all singers may benefit from both ingredient combos.

*Podium Back and Forth*

Going back and forth in a free form share of the podium can be the trickiest dish to not burn on the bottom. Some important preferences for both instructors to establish include "While I'm at the podium and you hear something from the ensemble you'd like to address, please jump in and contribute."—OR—"While I'm at the podium and you hear something from the ensemble you'd like to address, please don't jump in. I will invite your feedback when I'm ready." Use a stopwatch (or a kitchen timer) to structure how long each instructor has to work. Be able to say and stick to "I'd like to take three minutes to work this next section."

*Self-Guided Learning*

Having an individual voice teacher in the rehearsal helps facilitate individual growth, but so does fostering autonomous learning. Individuals in a group need the chance to respond to personal questions including: "What challenges do you want to work on in this piece," "What did you notice during the last run-through," and "What does this piece mean to you?" However, when rehearsal time is limited, these methods can be effective instead:

- Take a moment for each person to respond to the question in his or her own heads.
- Ask each person to turn to their neighbor and discuss their response.
- Create interactive warm-up and music learning games that involve choices and autonomy so that each person feels in charge of and responsible for their own singing.

RECIPE

# Becoming a Master Chef: The Professional Choral Singer

*Craig Hella Johnson*

The choral and vocal canon are vast and continually developing; comprising some of the largest and oldest repertory in history. Equally as vast are the capabilities of the human voice and the possibilities to develop a collective experience through ensemble performances of this ever-expanding repertoire. These experiences occur with singers of all ages in schools, colleges, community ensembles, and now, professional choral ensembles. We are fortunate to be establishing practices and building this viable career option, professional choral singing. In this setting, professional singers are able to come together and utilize their talents, training, and dedication to fully realize a composer's intentions and bring that unique story to an audience. This is achieved through creating a culture of "oneness," and an understanding of what this career brings to the world.[1]

**INGREDIENTS:**
Vocal training
An understanding of one's instrument
Musicianship & sight-reading skills
Passion
Curiosity
Flexibility
A dedicated travel schedule
A sense of humor

**SERVES:**
Singers, voice teachers, choral directors, and the audience.

There is an instant, indescribable "joy" that occurs when singers come together to share their musical and vocal gifts in a collaborative performance project. Within the professional choral context, it's an opportunity to make music at a very high level of artistry, and offers a higher potential of fully realizing music scores through love and attention to the choral art. Similar to becoming a master chef, the career path of a professional singer involves training, skill-building, intricacy and fine-tuning, and a generosity of spirit.

1. First, be sure students know professional choral singing is something they can aspire to and is a viable career option. Although this work requires a dedicated travel schedule to perform with multiple ensembles around the world, singers can indeed make a living as a professional singer.

1 This recipe was created from a phone interview between the author and editor.

- A typical paid, professional choral performance opportunity is a weeklong residency. Singers arrive an on Sunday and rehearse until Wednesday. Culminating performances occur either Thursday-Saturday or Friday-Sunday.
- Singers arrive fully prepared to the performance week so that time is spent on finding each other as an ensemble, and shaping, refining, and creating an interpretative perspective, or "voice," for each composition within the concert program.

2. Inspire students with a set of values that reflects diversity of expression and styles. Voice teachers can help introduce young singers to a wide variety of vocal offerings. We can't only rely on past traditions when singing was only thought of in certain ways and contexts. There is an immeasurable amount of music and styles to listen to today; utilize all the digital resources available.
3. Break down the stereotype that there is only one path to a life of singing. Do so by modeling your own curiosity and interests in a variety of music.
4. Help build a foundational vocal technique and teach students to not only know their instrument, but what they are doing with it.
5. Guide students towards various organizations and companies to find audition opportunities. Have students contact current singers within an organization for information.
6. Help students understand what skills and dispositions artistic directors are looking for in singers. Singers that:
   - Have a great sense of self-awareness and know their own instrument's (their voice) capabilities and weaknesses.
   - Have an evenness in their voice throughout all registers from top to bottom and bottom to top.
   - Have terrific sight-reading skills, with an attention to detail akin to that of string quartet. In essence, the ensemble can be thought of as a vocal chamber ensemble.
   - Have great "listening" ears, a refined sense of intonation within their own melodic line and within the vertical sonorities of the ensemble.
   - Can prepare repertoire with notes, rhythms, text, contextual research learned, and fit their voice into the repertoire ahead of the first rehearsal in a performance week.
   - Are flexible and adaptable musically and vocally.
   - Are collaborative and able to hear and balance one's own sound with a colleague's sound.
   - Are curious and willing to play with range and spectrum of the voice to serve the musical requirements of the repertoire.
   - Are interested in crossing the centuries, moving from Renaissance to Contemporary, or Baroque to Romantic.
   - Have a willingness to try new things and a "yes-kind" of curiosity. Singers should be willing to try something that might not be their first instinct or process.
   - Have a sense of humor.
   - Are gifted and kind.

When people are singing, often what is revealed is their most honest, open, and authentic selves. Professional choral singing offers an opportunity for a career engaging and exploring the voice and living in the joy of singing.

RECIPE

# Delectable Diction and Dialect in the Negro Spiritual

*LaToya Lain*

African American singers of classical music are expected to promote and preserve the Negro spiritual through concerts and recitals. However, this should be the responsibility of all American singers. The Negro spiritual is the oldest and most substantial paradigm of American folk song. It is an integral thread of the fabric that has woven the history of this country. The Negro spiritual is the musical styles and traditions of the enslaved African combined with the European musical aesthetic to create the sole foundation of American song. The enslaved Africans developed a dialect that could communicate the greatest amount of information in the fewest words. Dialect addresses what is spoken. Diction examines pronunciation. With this recipe, you will learn the dialect, diction, and performance practices of the American Negro spiritual.

**INGREDIENTS:**

A heaping of historical context
A pinch of consonant clusters
1 cup of minced definite articles
1/8 cup of chopped indefinite articles
1/2 cup of blended syllabic stress
1/4 cup of shredded final consonants
An abundant access to recordings of "the greats"

**SERVES:**

All singers who love to sing and want to share the story of Americans and the first American song form.

**Directions:**

With any piece of music, voice teachers should always begin with researching the historical context of the piece. Have singers look for information on the composer, the year it was written, and, if applicable, the author of the text. Please note, since spirituals were mostly passed down through the oral tradition, locating the name of the librettist is virtually impossible. Singers should investigate the types of spirituals, such as "code songs," "work songs," "social folk songs," "liturgical songs," and "songs of protest." Code songs such as "Steal Away" and "Wade in the Water" have hidden messages. Work songs were songs that the slaves sang to help keep the rhythm of the laborious activity. Liturgical songs told the stories of the bible and celebrated religion. Knowing this background information will inform subtext and allow singers to adequately deliver the text with meaning.

Only a "pinch" of consonant clusters at the end of a word is needed, as the common practice is to drop the last consonant. For example, "test" becomes "tes" and "hand" becomes "han." Dropped final consonant clusters include -st, -sp, -sk, -zd, -ft, -vd, -nd, -ld, -pt, and -kt. "Done found my lost sheep" will sound "Don' foun' mah los' sheep."

With one cup of minced definite articles, "th" at the beginning of a word becomes "d;" the word "that," is sung "dat." For example, "Talk about a child dat do love Jesus." The word "the," is sung "de." An example of this is "Nobody know de trouble I see..." "R" and "l" consonants are pronounced when they begin a word, but when they are the final consonant, they are neutralized when following a vowel; the word "sister" becomes "sis-tuh." Final "b," "d," and "g" often become unvoiced when located at the end of a word. For example, "How lon' de train been gone?" 1/8 of a cup of chopped indefinite articles eliminates the word "an." In spirituals, it is customary to sing "a," pronounced "uh," even if the following word begins with a vowel.

Blended syllabic stress gives the singer permission to compress or add syllables to words. A great example of syllabic compression is dropping the "a" in "about." For example, "Been a long time a-talkin' 'bout my trials here below." Also notice in this example, the word "talking" received an added syllable and became "a-talkin'." Another example of adding syllables can be found in "Come down angels, a-trouble de watuh, let God's saints a-come in."

Lastly, singers need an abundant supply of recordings of the greats. Studying the style of spirituals as heard in the recordings of Marian Anderson, Paul Robeson, Roland Hayes, William Warfield, and Leontyne Price will not only train a singer's ear to the performance style of the spiritual, but these recordings will also inspire singers to make these great songs their own!

"Of course, it is not necessary to be an expert in Negro dialect to sing the spirituals, but most of them lose their charm when they are sung in straight English. Any performer of non-African ethnic background singing the spiritual in original dialect must understand that original dialect is not a comment upon him or herself as a performer, but acknowledgement of the linguistic qualities that are authentic to the genre." — James Weldon Johnson

RECIPE

# Utilizing the Natural Prosody of Speech in Cooking Up Hot Jazz, Pop, and "Patter" Tunes

*Rachel Lebon*

Some of the most challenging songs to internalize and perform effectively are "wordy" song selections wherein the melody is woven around the words, usually *many* of them, and at a "burning" tempo. Referred to as up-tempo or patter tunes, this repertoire can be very challenging to perform, but also very rewarding.

Patter tunes are represented in all musical styles, and set against a rhythmic groove. The challenge for the vocalist is to clearly project the lyrics with a sense of spontaneity and awareness of the prosody of language, that is, a sensitivity to the rhythm, intonation and stress of the lyrics as spoken. These elements are the essential ingredients that enable vocalists to be clearly understood and align with the music's rhythmic palette. Attention to the language in music enables singers to effectively "sell" a patter tune regardless of the musical style or idiom.

**INGREDIENTS:**
A sense of prosody
Articulatory skills
Strong rhythmic sense
Micro-phrasing

**SERVES:**
Jazz vocalists, jazz vocal ensembles, pop vocalists, and musical theatre singers.

**Strategies for Effectively Serving up Patter Tunes**

The essential ingredients in effectively serving up a patter tune is to understand the elements of prosody, that is, an awareness of the elements of rhythm, intonation, and stress or accent of language. Additionally, students need tongue flexibility for intelligibility and clear articulation, a strong rhythmic sense with the ability to maintain fast tempi without rushing, and should also understand the concept of "micro-phrasing," that is, giving attention to inner phrase ideas within the larger phrase as if the ideas are occurring to you spontaneously, rather than pre-planned.

Strategies to achieve this include:

1. First, have singers explore micro-phrasing, or the attention to inner phrase ideas within a larger phrase. The phrase "Sometimes you have to think big!" can be

expressed as three ideas or micro-phrases, e.g., "Sometimes, you have to think… big!" Placing focus on the inner-phrases can result in subtle pauses and changes in dynamics and vocal color, thereby clearly bringing the phrase ideas to the listener.

2. Having vocalists speak the lyrics of the song with "attitude," like a monologue, using the rhythm, intonation, and stress corresponding to the lyrics of the song.
3. This approach facilitates memorization which helps communicate the song lyrics, enabling the ingredients to blend together harmoniously.
4. Next, the lyrics can now be stirred into the melody. The prosody of the language should fold into the contour of the melody and sound spontaneous.
5. Having assembled the ingredients, vocalists may discover that attention to rhythm and speech prosody enables singers to project the lyrics and flavor of the song with facility, notwithstanding the challenging tempo, since rhythm, intonation, and stress elements of the language are working in tandem.
6. With practice, the lyrics will be served comfortably up-tempo and align with the melody and harmony, enabling singers to engage the audience and "sell the song."

While some of the old standards below may not necessarily correspond with every singer's *fach*, they can serve as "exercises" to develop the ability to sound spontaneous and work with the prosody of the language while projecting effectively

**Female Musical Theatre Patter:**

"Everybody Say's Don't": Up-tempo; demands strong articulation.

"Johnny One Note": Wide-range; contrasting B section with melodic leaps.

"Wherever He Ain't": Wide-range; requires strong articulation and sense of phrasing to effectively communicate lyrics; incorporates upper belt.

"The Miller's Son": Slow, introspective verse prior to B section, which develops into a contrasting triplet rhythmic feel that accentuates the lyrics on beats 1 and 4. Entails strong dramatic skills.

**Males: Popular Music and Jazz:**

"Never Giving Up" by Al Jarreau: Quasi Samba, ideal for developing facility with fast patter. Demands wide vocal range with lyrics as the most important element.

"Cloudburst" by Lambert, Hendricks, and Ross Trio: Jazz up-tempo standard that is ideal in practicing fast patter. In ensemble arrangements, the vocalise section is often performed as a solo.

"Confirmation" by Manhattan Transfer: Up-tempo; works well for solo and/or group.

"Bopblicity" by John Hendricks: Song works well for soloist as well as with an ensemble or Trio, à la Lambert, Hendricks, and Ross.

There's much to be learned as a vocalist performing patter tunes in *any* idiom because a comfortable union of lyrics and music results in presentational skills that are guaranteed to effectively communicate patter to an appreciative audience.

RECIPE

# Stretching the Dough: A Heather Lyle Vocal Yoga Method® Singer's Warm-Up

*Heather Lyle*

Yoga combines a combination of flexibility and strengthening exercises connected to breathing, which makes it perfect for the singer. In yoga, rounded body positions are better for sounding high notes, and arched body positions are better for low notes. Singing while doing a *vinyasa* yoga flow series assists the voice in releasing freely from the body in its natural, authentic form. This short yoga sequence, or recipe, is from yoga therapy and can be used by any body type.

**INGREDIENTS:**
One yoga mat, nice to have but not necessary
Clothes you can move in

**SERVES:**
All singers.

Try the following steps with your singers:

1. Start your yoga sequence in mountain pose (*tadasana*) by standing with your feet parallel, hip distance apart. Bring your hands together in prayer pose with your palms together at your heart. Firm your thigh muscles and lift your kneecaps but keep your belly soft.
2. Inhale and stretch your arms out to the side and overhead touching palm to palm. Take two full breaths with your arms overhead feeling the breath expanding under your ribcage.
3. On the third breath, reach your hands upward and exhale as you bring your arms down and back to your heart. You can repeat this a few times, if you'd like. It wakes up the breath beautifully.
4. Once again, inhale as you bring your arms overhead but this time exhale with a relaxed "ah" as you bring your arms out to the side; like an airplane folding down into a standing full forward bend (*uttanasana*) with the arms falling to the floor. If you have tight hamstrings, bend your knees so that the back can relax and stretch.
5. Inhale and bring your hands onto your shins as you lengthen your back, rising up halfway into *ardha uttanasana* (half-hang over).
6. Fold back over toward the ground while sounding on "ah." While hanging over, see if you can feel the lower back expand with breath.
7. Walk your hands out in front of you, bring your knees down on to the mat, and come into a neutral "table top" position. Have your wrists directly below your

shoulders and your knees directly below your hips. Inhale and relax the belly around the navel.

8. Inhale and lift your chest and head upward while lifting your sit-bones toward the ceiling into cow posture (*bitilasana*). The middle of the body will sink down toward the floor.
9. Exhale on "sh" as you gently engage your abdominal muscles and follow the length of the exhalation as you come into a fully arched, scared halloween cat posture (*marjariasana*). Move your spine between cow and cat a few times to wake up the spine and then try exhaling on a sung "shaw" instead of an unvoiced "sh."
10. Tuck your toes under and come into downward dog (*adho mukha svanasana*), an upside down "V" position. This posture is amazing to expand the breath capacity of the singer, so try breathing in a variety of ways before singing in this posture. While in downward dog, the core is once again very active, so consciously release the belly around the navel and breathe into it.
11. Now try breathing into the sides of the torso expanding the waist outward. Try breathing just into the middle back, expanding the lower portion of the ribcage and see, as you add more air, if you can expand the back all the way up to the shoulder blades arching up into a hump as the ribs open up. By opening up the back, the lungs are stretched in areas that are usually not active. The more flexibility and mobility in the ribcage, the more the lungs can expand and increase lung power. Feel free to come down on to your hands and knees and then go back up into the posture.
12. Downward dog is comfortable to sing in. You will find that the middle and upper registers of your voice are easy to get into. Sing some high notes on "woo." Try sliding the voice up and down the scale (glissando) and see if you can feel the voice coming from the base of the spine, traveling up the spine and ending in the head on the highest notes. If your tongue is tight try wiggling it out of your mouth as you sound.
13. Bend your knees and come down to the mat, or if you are more athletic you can come into a push-up position called plank (*kumbhakasana*), and slowly lower to the ground. If you chose plank, stay in it for a few minutes and try singing short, speech-level or low tones on a "wah," while engaging your abdominal muscles for both physical and vocal support.
14. Now lie on your belly for an arch. Put your palms under your shoulders elbows in, or farther forward or even spread your arms out in a "V" shape so your hands are closer to the corners of the mat.
15. Keep your legs and buttocks firm and inhale as you reach slightly forward with your body as you push up into cobra. While in cobra, relax the belly and feel the breath dropping into the whole front of the torso and sound or sing short, speech-level or low tones on "wuh" "wah" or "fuh" or even woof! See if you can feel the abdominal muscles engage as you make sound. This is a great posture for working on your lower register.
16. For your final posture, move your rear-end back towards your feet and come into child's pose (*balasana*), with your arms spread forward in front of you. Child's pose is a very nice pose to hum or sing high "mews" to cool down the voice.
17. Slowly come into a seated position and end the sequence by singing an "om" on any pitch you choose while bringing your palms back to prayer pose. Thank yourself for the gift of your voice and feel gratitude for all life has brought you. Your voice and body should feel warmed up for singing.

RECIPE

# Thyme to Take the Next Step and Dance

*Valerie Lippoldt Mack*

The *King And I* was set in Bangkok in the 1860's and to Anna, an early music educator, the King's invitation of "Shall we dance?" might have been a legitimate question. In the 21st century, it is purely rhetorical. With the popularity of the dance and voice reality shows, our world is inundated with movement and music. Musicians realize that physical movement adds life to choral music, both in rehearsal and in performance. Yet, many first-year educators are thrust into the show choir and musical theatre world without a firm knowledge of what is involved and where to go for help. Movement and music are closely related, and the relationship provides synergy for everyone involved. So now what?

**INGREDIENTS:**
Voice teachers
Ensemble directors
Singers
"Thyme"

**SERVES:**
Ensemble members and audiences alike with energy-driven rehearsals and performances. Singers will maintain vocal quality when adding movement. Anyone can take their program a "step" up if they put in the "thyme!"

Simply stated, choreography, when used tastefully can complement and enhance the educational and entertainment value of the music. Singing comes first and good choreography never gets in the way of good singing. Of course, any movement that detracts from the vocal line or choral sound should be avoided. Generally, motion attracts attention, and yet, continuous motion is just as boring as no motion at all. There must be a balance—but exactly how do we find that balance and get started?

First, and foremost, when selecting music, assess the musical and dance talents of your students. Identify your student's strengths and weaknesses. Highlight your students' versatility and let them shine. Make age appropriate musical choices and yet, be sure to challenge the singer and the audience member. Be relentless in your search for suitable programming. All good works of art have unity as well as variety. Performers and audience members deserve the very best when it comes to programming.

The vocal style should match the choreography. Use choreography that is authentic and stylistic. Musicians wouldn't think about performing a French chanson in barbershop style. Ridiculous you say, and yet that is what often happens when choreography is added. Just how does one remain loyal to the music and dance style? In the day of Siri and Google, it is easier than ever to research dance styles by accessing the web. Utilize all available resources, including videos, photos, dance teachers, workshops, summer camps, and your students. Be sure to respect and be inspired by the creator, but avoid copying entire sections of choreography for copyright reasons.

Keep it simple! Many times, we make things more complicated than necessary. Risers, boxes, chairs, stools, ladders, and other dimensional props create unique pictures and dimensions. A simple change of a tableau helps the audience and the singer stay involved in the show. Costume changes, wigs, props, adding and subtracting lighting, dance features, and formation changes are a few ways to add an element of surprise and/or motion to the music. Rehearse facial and performance-level energy from the beginning. Insist on good posture and energetic movements at all times as practice makes permanent.

Use lyrics to help coordinate the movement, but avoid pantomime unless you want comedy—or trite choreography. A helpful musical game is the "TV monitor game." Video a rehearsal and then ask ensemble members to watch the rehearsal without any sound. Can singers decipher the storyline by watching the choreography? Is it clean choreography or too busy? Play the recording a second time, but this time turn off the picture (or ask singers to shut their eyes) and listen to the number. Is the diction clean and crisp? Is the movement getting in the way of the lyrics? Use this lesson as a written assignment by having students critique his or her performances and then compare and share the results.

Voice instructors should use the same movement techniques in the voice studio. Use choreographed moves (i.e., throwing roses in the air, "throw" a football, flop over like a ragdoll, pretend to dog paddle, paint a barn with super glue) to help free the voice and add energy to the sound. Choreography should match the tempo changes and the vocal dynamic choices in each piece. These movement techniques can be used in the voice studio and then applied on stage.

When all else fails . . . hire a choreographer! Don't sign up the local Zumba teacher or PE instructor unless he or she has an understanding of vocal production. Check around to find professionals that comprehend the union of music and dance. Dream big. If you can imagine it, it can be achieved with the right choreographic tools and the right people.

I wish for all of us to be like Anna that we can listen and learn from those around us. Help us not be stubborn like the King who was stuck in tradition and self-absorption, but instead enjoy "Getting to know" each other and trust one another as we make performances more exciting for the students and audience members alike. In the end, it truly is about making the best of the journey and not just reaching the destination. Good luck with your musical endeavors and let us choose to take the next step and DANCE!

RECIPE

# Vocal Exercises: Using the Correct Ingredients in the Correct Order

*Brian Manternach*

My oldest sister is famous in our family for the light, fluffy Baking Powder Biscuits she used to make that perfectly accompanied hot soup on cold winter days. On one occasion, however, she mistakenly replaced the title ingredient with baking *soda*. While these two ingredients function similarly in recipes, they are not always interchangeable, as we found out when the rock-hard Baking Soda Biscuits were pulled from the oven.

Vocal exercises have different purposes, too. If you want to increase your range, for instance, exercises designed to improve agility may not help you reach that goal. Therefore, developing a recipe for vocal practice requires knowing how different vocalises function so you can select the right ones and implement them in the appropriate order.

**INGREDIENTS:**

Vocal exercises that:

1. Warm up the body and voice
2. Build specific elements of vocal technique
3. Incorporate sections of vocal repertoire
4. Serve as a vocal cool-down

**SERVES:**

Those seeking to develop strategies for efficient and effective vocal practice.

Physical stretches not only prepare and "awaken" the muscles of the body for singing but also help shift mental focus and attention as we transition from other activities to the act of singing. After a brief routine of full-body stretches, try an exercise that exaggerates the breath cycle: breathe in for five counts, suspend the air with an open glottis (do not "hold" the air) for five counts, and then exhale for five counts. Encourage feelings of looseness and release in areas prone to unnecessary tension like the neck, jaw, and tongue. Observe your body's balance between inhalations that are primarily wide (reflecting the motion of the external intercostal muscles) and primarily low (reflecting diaphragmatic movement).

*The Vocal Athlete* authors Wendy D. Leborgne and Marci Rosenberg explain that warm-ups should be gentle exercises designed to "get things moving."[1] These are differentiated from vocalises, which are used to address specific technical issues. Therefore, your first vocal exercises should explore the middle portion of your range at a medium dynamic level.

1 Wendy D. Leborgne and Marci Rosenberg, *The Vocal Athlete* (San Diego: Plural Publishing, 2014), 250.

This encourages blood flow and oxygen to muscles, raises the temperature of the muscles (literally warms them up!), and increases muscular flexibility and range of motion.[2]

Semi-occluded vocal tract exercises (SOVTEs) are effective vocalises that bring the muscles of phonation into balance, reduce vocal effort, and coordinate phonation with airflow. Examples include lip trills, tongue trills, humming on an [m], [n], or [ŋ], and singing into straws of various sizes. Use these exercises on several note patterns, and then try going back and forth from an SOVTE to a vowel. For example, sing a five-note scale through a straw and follow it immediately with a five-note scale on an [o].

After this work, you are ready to expand the vocal range of the exercises and target specific aspects of your technique. For a useful list of vocalises, read Dr. Ingo Titze's well-circulated article, "The Five Best Vocal Warm-Up Exercises."[3] Many of the exercises in the article can also be used for strengthening vocal range and flexibility.

In fact, most exercises can be used to warm up *and* build the voice, depending on how they are carried out. A five-note scale can be a productive warm-up if used in the middle part of your range at a medium dynamic level and on a lip trill. Used in the range around your "break" on an [i] vowel and then an [a] vowel, it now becomes an exercise designed to develop the specific skill of singing smoothly through the *passaggio*.

Next, take challenging excerpts from the repertoire you are learning and turn them into vocal exercises by isolating them out of context. Try singing the passages on [ŋ] or on your favorite vowel, temporarily omitting the words. You may try singing the phrase while focusing on just one technical element, like maintaining freedom at the jaw or keeping an even, legato line.

Lastly, many pedagogues advocate cool-down exercises after intense vocal work. Just as biscuits cool down after coming out of the oven, it can be a good idea to cool the voice down at the end of a long practice session. In a research study by Kari Ragan, singers reported that their voices felt better and more relaxed after cool-down exercises that included straw phonation, humming, and singing on a "floaty [u]."[4]

There are so many elements of technique to address as we build our vocal capabilities. Knowing the purpose of each exercise can help you systematically plan out a progressive recipe for a successful practice session.

2 Ibid.

3 Ingo R. Titze, "The Five Best Vocal Warm-Up Exercises," *Journal of Singing* 57, no. 3 (2001): 51–52.

4 Kari Ragan, "The Impact of Vocal Cool-down Exercises: A Subjective Study of Singers' and Listeners' Perceptions," *Journal of Voice* 30, no. 6 (2016): 764.e1–764.e9.

RECIPE

# Cooking/Singing with the Letter "R"

*Lori McCann*

The letter "r" is consistently problematic in lyric diction until thoroughly understood and consistently practiced. This will be an international recipe for the articulation of the semi-vowel, glide, and consonant "r" in lyric diction.

**INGREDIENTS:**
Air
Tongue
Jaw
Alveolar Ridge
Hard Palate
Soft Palate
IPA
Song Text

**SERVES:**
Italian, French, German and English.

Flip: [ɾ], roll: [R/r], retroflex: [ɹ], or remove: [ ] refer to "consonant-r" pronunciations in the four primary singing languages—Italian, French, German, English. You will also encounter "vowel-r" pronunciations represented with the following symbols:

- [ɝ] [ɜr] stressed "uhr" sound in American English (fur, heard, third, word, bird)
- [ɚ] [ər] unstressed "uhr" sound in American English (*brother*)
- [ɜ] "r-less uhr" sound in British English (*bird, no retroflex tongue*)
- [ɐ] "schwa + r" in British English (most often "-er" endings; *father*)
- [ʁ] "r-colored schwa" in German that my students have dubbed the *Schwar*

When one encounters the letter "r" in a song text there are choices to be made about the pronunciation.

1. What language is the piece in?
   a. Where does the "r" come in the word?
   b. What letters precede it?
   c. What letters follow it?
2. What genre is the piece in?
3. What is the accompaniment? (orchestra, piano, eight cellos . . . )
4. What is the venue and acoustic in which the piece will be performed?

Once you have reliably answered these questions, you are ready to begin. The following instructions will serve you well depending on whether you will cook Italian, French, German, British or North American English food.

**Italy:**
When cooking/singing in Italian, you have simple and straight forward "consonant-r" rules, and the letter "r" never masquerades as a semi-vowel or glide in this most sing-able of languages.

1. Use the "flipped r" [ɾ], when it is found between two vowels (*cara*)
2. Use the "rolled or trilled r" [r] or [rr] for all other positions in a word (*credi, pur*)

   Exception: At high altitudes/tessitura you may need to substitute a "flipped r" [ɾ] when final in a word.

Warning: You may never substitute "rolled r" when the recipe calls for a "flipped r" or you will get an entirely different result/word. (*caro* vs. *carro*)

**France:**
France is also home to one of the great cuisines of the world. They too use a simplified version of their complicated spoken "rolled uvular r" for cooking/art song or opera singing.

1. In all cases you merely flip the "r" [ɾ]. One tap of the tongue is sufficient. (*coeur*)

   Note: The mid-tongue "rolled uvular-r" is used for speech, popular music and cabaret.

**Germany:**
In German, the spoken "r" is also uvular as it is in France. It is produced even further back then the French spoken "r," and therefore, we do not use it for lyric diction. However, the German "uvular-r," produced with the back of the tongue and the uvula, is used in popular song and spoken dialogue.

For singing German art song and opera we use the "flipped r" [ɾ], and the "rolled or trilled r" [r] or [rr] as in Italian.

Consonant "r":

1. Flipped "r" will suffice just about anywhere there is an "r" (*ihre, vor, Ruhe*)
2. Rolled "r" is used for emphasis, especially at the beginning of a word for added flavor! (*roll, rot, Reihn*)

Vowel "r":

1. Final "r" can be omitted in words with a long [ɑ:] (i.e., Wahr = [vɑ:].
2. Central vowel [ʁ], or what I like to call the *Schwar*—"schwa-colored r."
   This is equivalent to the British [ɐ]. Both are sometimes used for *-er* endings (*aber, anders, die Schwester*), and especially in one syllable words or after a closed long vowel at the end of a word or before a consonant. (*der, dir, vier, die Uhr, fährst*) [de:ɐ] [di:ɐ] [fi:ʁ] [di ˀu:ʁ] [fɛ:ʁst]. You will find both of these IPA transcriptions [de:ʁ] or [de:ɐ]in various cook/diction books.

   Note: Although it is acceptable to use the [ʁ] or [ɐ] in modern German diction, up until the mid-20th century, only "flipped-r" was used in German lyric diction. Some teachers and singers still prefer this.

Warning: One must never substitute the American "retroflex-r" sound for the "schwa colored-r" when cooking/singing in German.

**North America:**
The North American English "retroflex r" [ɹ] is particularly problematic for singing and should be used mindfully in most classical styles of singing. Singers and cooks must be careful not to use too much of it, or linger too long in the retroflex tongue position, lest it spoil the resonance or intelligibility of the text. However, it is used almost exclusively, as in speech, in musical theater and popular styles of singing such as jazz, pop, rock, and especially country. It is considered a semi-vowel or semi-consonant and often functions as a glide.

In addition to the mindful use of the "retroflex r" [ɹ], North American English singers also employ the following for the letter "r" in English:

Vowel "r":

1. Use the "schwa-colored-r," [ɐ] as used by British English speakers and singers.
2. Drop the final "r's" altogether to soften the harshness of the delivery of this North American "r" sound, and to improve their resonance.
3. They also employ the "r-less uhr" sound as in the word "bird" pronounced as the British would [bɜd] as opposed to [bɝd]/[bɜɹd].

Semi-consonant or glide "r":

1. Use the standard "flipped-r" [ɾ] initial in a word, or especially between vowels and in consonant clusters.
2. May even choose the "rolled-r" [r] initial in a word or in a consonant cluster for emphasis and carrying power.

Proper use of the letter "r" can add distinctive flavor, flare or pizzazz to any recipe/aria. Just be sure that you check the requirements of each country of origin for your song or aria before choosing which one to use!

*Buon appetit! Bon appétit! Guten appetit,* Enjoy your meal!

RECIPE

# Blending Batters: A Recipe for the Coaching Teacher

*Samantha Miller*

The voice teacher and the vocal coach both serve vital roles in the training of professional singers. Although each has some ingredients in common, the differing proportions of the ingredients in each recipe give each one its own distinct taste and purpose. This is why singers are encouraged to have consistent individualized sessions with a vocal teacher and a vocal coach.

However, many young singers studying at the collegiate level or directly entering into the entertainment industry either do not have the opportunity to experience this, or understand the importance of having individualized instruction from these two specialists. At the university level, it is often the collaborative pianist (coach) who is missing from this equation. In such cases, there is a need for the voice teacher to blend recipes and take on the "coaching" responsibilities inside the studio. While blending recipes is not a normal procedure, it is, for the good of our students, one that we as teachers should not refuse.

**INGREDIENTS:**
1/4 c. Pride
2 c. Individual Expertise, Knowledge, and Education
1/2 c. Current Industrial Trends
1/2 c. Current Pedagogical Trends
2 tbsp. Language and Linguistic Refinement

**SERVES:**
The voice teacher whose students do not have frequent access to a vocal coach.

**Instructions:**
Combine ingredients by using the following steps to make sure that your singers look good, sound good, and present themselves as consistent, accurate, and expressive in the appropriate genre, style, and language they are performing.

1. Take some of your pride and swallow it! Technical instruction in a voice lesson is of utmost importance, but the musical style, language consistency, and performance application cannot be neglected, as it will put the singer at a disadvantage when competing for opportunities. Taking on this responsibility in your own instruction can help bridge the gap for young singers.

2. Next, sift all of your personal knowledge and expertise. This sifting separates the information that is well known from the information that needs reviewing. There may be some stylistic, artistic and even technical concepts that have been forgotten or blurred with time, especially if working with one gender, *fach*, or style more consistently than others. The "coaching teacher" must know when a stylistic characteristic is appropriate and be able to physiologically understand and describe how to create it. For example, if you believe it appropriate to use straight-tone on a specific pitch, the result is achieved quickly and adequately by the student if it is clearly explained to them how to produce it. Once the knowledge that needs to be reviewed is identified, you can refresh what is lacking by listening to and watching great singers, both new and old, of all styles and genres, and by reading stylistic guides and research.
3. Music is constantly evolving and it is important for a teacher to know what is trending, even in classical circles, because those auditioning and hiring singers have constantly evolving visions of the types of singers that they wish to hire. Find these trends by interviewing singers you know who are successful in the industry and by keeping connected in professional circles. Where are these students going to school? What programs are these students participating in? What are the audition requirements for programs, agents, roles and recording labels? This, combined with your knowledge will give your singers an advantage in the audition process.
4. Be open to learning new concepts and growing as a teacher. Find joy and purpose in new research in the pedagogical world of voice, which is readily available to you on your computer, phone, or tablet at any time. Also, find what is stylistically appropriate in current musical genres and combine it with your own personal pedagogical style. Finding new ways to teach and new styles to try will keep you relevant, yet consistent as a coaching teacher.
5. To maintain consistency, the coaching teacher must keep diction and linguistic knowledge accurate and fresh. Learning or refreshing diction "chops" is about more than just retaining the "sound," but also about studying features of the articulators and their roles in enunciation in each language; this helps our singers sound authentic and appear polished and prepared.

RECIPE

# Flavor Profiles and Repertoire

*Jeremy Ryan Mossman*

There are as many musical styles on Broadway as there are culinary options at a buffet and repertoire surfaces daily on YouTube like a new spin on mac & cheese. To help a student find fitting music, you need to know their preferred buffet stations, if they prefer sweet or savory, and their tolerance for spice. Imagine what they would cook if they had the skills. The more details you know about our students' palates, the more you can help them become masters of their own cooking.

**INGREDIENTS:**
1 Heap Internet
1 Cup Curiosity

**SERVES:**
Teachers working with musical theatre performers.

### Finding *the* Song

Here's a recipe for finding repertoire as a team effort between you and a student that should generate a handful of options in one sitting:

1. Find *Doppelgängers*
   a. Have your student ask their friends who they remind them of on Broadway, past and present.
   b. Find them on the "Internet Broadway Database" or "Playbill Vault" to see what roles they've played, who also played those parts and what other parts they've played.
2. Take the research to YouTube, paying attention for patterns such as:
   a. Composers who seem to write well for the range and/or style.
   b. Eras that feel genuine for the student.
   c. The archetype that stands out across several songs.

### The Main Dish — Your Student

I have found that assigning songs based on the roles students would be cast as usually lines up well with their vocal abilities. This also prepares them for future opportunities. Finding characters that share a story with your students will make it easier for them to personalize their interpretation.

"I Am/I Want" songs are usually found early in the first act of a musical where the protagonist informs the audience what's in store for their journey. Because these songs focus on a character's development rather than plot, they allow a student to bring a song to life using their own thoughts, feelings, and experiences. These songs can be so adaptable to each performer that they can also become overdone like "Pulled," "Corner of the Sky," and "Part of That World." Luckily, there are a lot of musicals, and almost all of them have an "I Am/I Want" song! If you get a whiff that a song you or your student find are potentially overdone, find an alternate option. Though every performer ought to be serving a unique interpretation of every song, at the end of a long day of auditions, it's hard to recall individuality from performances of the same songs. It's also wise to avoid songs that have been made iconic by performers. If you don't want your students to be compared to Barbra Streisand then they shouldn't sing "I'm The Greatest Star," or "Not For The Life Of Me."

**The Cutting Board**

Your student may ask you for help making cuts, often 16 or 32 bars. The first thing you need to know is "16 bars" does not always mean exactly 16 bars of music! It is a phrase of music as well as a complete thought. Likewise, 32 bars mean two phrases, or two complete thoughts. It usual aligns with a verse or a verse & chorus, respectively. If you aren't sure, time your cuts at no more than 45 seconds per 16 bars.

A cut doesn't have to be exactly as the music was written—it's ok to cut out bars or phrases and splice sections together as long as the cuts make sense musically and form logical sentences. If the song is very well known, consider if internal cutting will be distracting. It's a good idea to have an introduction that's two bars or less.

When in doubt, less is more—don't serve a meal if someone's looking for a sample.

**The Musical Presentation**

Most accompanists would agree that music is best in a binder with the music double-sided to minimize page turns. They tend to not like plastic page protectors, even the "glare free" ones.

Use a highlighter to direct the accompanist's eye to things in the music that you want them to observe such as tempo, key, or feel changes, when the music slows or accelerates, pauses or held notes, etc. Make it as easy as possible for someone to sight-read the music and support the intended choices.

**Conclusion**

What matters the most is how a performer connects with the audience. If they have high quality ingredients that have been prepared appropriately and seasoned just right, they will serve a artistic meal to remember.

"Anything you do, let it come from you. Then it will be new. Give us more to see..."
— Stephen Sondheim

Give us more to taste.

RECIPE

# A Recipe for Alignment

*Dawn Wells Neely*

Singers are never separated from their instruments, and every aspect of their lifestyle from diet to leisure activities may affect their sound. While teachers spend large amounts of time working on breath management and vocal resonance, a singer must have control over the body before vocal training may be fully mastered. Alignment refers to the relationship of one body part to another within the body. If one has poor posture while singing, body parts may be out of alignment. Not only must a singer have proper body alignment to allow for efficient breathing and ease of vocal production, but he or she must also be aware of changes in the body's alignment during singing in order to make adjustments.

**INGREDIENTS:**

A singer
A teacher to watch and help the singer assess the position of the body
Full-length mirror
Wall surface
Yoga mat
Kinesthetic awareness: Often enhanced through mind-body methods

**SERVES:**

The singer's body and confidence! With good alignment, the singer will be more comfortable and confident in practice and on the stage.

The singer should have a teacher who can deliver feedback on alignment through visual guidance and assessment. This instruction will help the singer strengthen his or her kinesthetic awareness. Releasing tension in the neck muscles will allow the head to lead and the rest of the body to follow. Therefore, the singer should start with aligning the body from the head downward. The ideal alignment of the body to ensure good posture can be imagined with a plumb line of gravity drawn down through the side of the body.

The singer should imagine a free and easy positioning of the head. The head sits at the top of the spine at the first cervical vertebra (the atlas) and on the second cervical vertebra (the axis). The skull balances on this joint, allowing it to move freely. The beginning of the spine is not located at the back of the head, but almost between the ears! The chin should be parallel to the floor. The crown of the head should be the focal point of upward direction. Using the full-length mirror, the singer should be sure to check that the head is not jutted too far forward, or pulled back in an exaggerated manner. Singers often try to thrust the head forward and stiffen the muscles in the neck to reach high notes or pull the head back and down for lower notes. These positions will only take the larynx out of its alignment and shorten the vocal tract.

The singer's sternum should be lifted with the shoulders positioned back and down, allowing the arms to hang loosely at the sides of the torso. The singer may imagine that the torso is lifting up from the hips rather than falling forward into a hunched over or slouched position. In addition to the teacher's feedback and visual cues from the mirror, the singer may also stand against a wall or lay down in the supine position on a yoga mat to feel the openness of the chest and shoulders without tension. Singing with the shoulders and upper back against a wall or on a yoga mat is encouraged to instill body alignment awareness.

With the torso upright, tilt the pelvis back and forth to find a position that is not too exaggerated. This positioning will allow the back to maintain its natural curves. The singer should be mindful to keep the back from swaying too much (top of the pelvis is tilted too far forward). The singer should not try to eliminate the natural curves of the spine by flattening or over-straightening the back (top of the pelvis is too tilted too far back). These curves are necessary to support the weight of the body. Use a mirror for visual awareness in addition to feedback from a teacher to find the best position of the pelvis.

The arches of the feet deliver the weight of the body from the center of the foot, outward. The singer should allow weight to be placed evenly on the balls of the feet and heels without putting too much weight onto one side of the body. This distribution is easy to maintain by keeping the legs shoulder width apart. The singer should keep the knees "soft" instead of constricted. By keeping the knees soft, the singer has flexibility in the legs to shift weight evenly downward and keep the body grounded. A grounded or centered body will be more adaptive to the subtle changes in alignment that take place during respiration for singing.

Mind-body methods like yoga, Alexander Technique, and the Feldenkrais Method, use awareness to enhance the kinesthetic perception of the body in space and during movement for ease of function. These methods are useful for the singer to become more aware of his/her alignment while singing. For further information on these mind-body methods, visit the following websites:

- The Yoga Alliance, www.yogaalliance.org
- The American Society for the Alexander Technique, www.amsatonline.org
- The Feldenkrais Institute, www.feldenkraisinstitute.org

An understanding and awareness of how the body is best aligned will allow the singer to use the body more easily and efficiently for singing. Proper alignment of the entire body, from the head down to the feet, will give the singer a sense of freedom and enable him or her to sing and perform with confidence.

RECIPE

# Recipes for Success: Developing a "Palate" for Assessment

*Corinne Ness*

Developing good assessment skills as an instructor is much akin to the chef developing a palate for flavors. Just as the chef must be able to appreciate acid and fat or salt and sweet, the voice instructor must develop a discriminating ear (and eye) to assess inefficient or inauthentic vocal recipes and to suggest ingredients that will help develop the vocal "flavors" of the student/artist. Teachers then need to make plans for instruction to meet the developmental needs of the student/artist. This is assessment.

**INGREDIENTS:**
A collaborative instructor
A curious student/artist
A good set of ears
A good set of eyes
Face-sized or full-length mirror
Paper and pencil, or computer for documenting assessment

**SERVES:**
Voice student development and instructional planning for teachers.

Most voice lessons are structured similarly—warm-ups, technical drills, and repertoire. Voice teachers make recommendations to adjust the vocal "recipe" for efficiency, style, or aesthetic aims. Assessment provides tools to new and experienced teachers for "taking stock" of vocal recipes and developing a discriminating palate for different vocal styles. New teachers can feel unprepared for this type of "taking stock" of the voice. Experienced teachers may have a sophisticated "palate" for a particular style, but may be less experienced in "taking stock" of unfamiliar musical "flavors." Like the cook attempting a new dish, the voice instructor must have a keen palate to identify ingredients, adjust proportions, and add flavors for a perfectly balanced recipe. Similarly, an assessment framework can organize and translate a teacher's intuition into a clear methodology. Assessment can be a tool for day-to-day studio activities, or a tool for setting goals for growth and determining student progress for academic grades or solo auditions. A simple paper and pencil or laptop can be used to "take stock" of the voice in key areas.

**Posture and Alignment.** The voice instructor's first assessment tool is the eye and the mirror. Student/artists can't help but bring part of the outside world into the lesson—tensions and postural habits that reflect their daily circumstances and tendencies. Teachers should look for any physical imbalance. Does a shoulder creep up, reflecting a tension? Does the jaw pull to one side, reflecting a tension? Identify the imbalances, and make adjustments. Many times, directing the student/artist's attention to the imbalance is all that is needed; they can recalibrate by focusing on creating symmetry and finding balance points.

**Breath Function.** Each vocal style, from *bel canto* to belt, requires a different approach to breath usage. Identifying the optimal breath usage is a key foundation to the vocalism. Teachers should assess whether the inhalation is high? Low? Sudden? Sustained? Does the exhalation have a feeling of suspension? Flow? Spin? What choice would be most efficient for the style being sung? Is there an efficient recoil breath at the end of each phrase? Providing student/artists with vocalises or song phrases that can be sung with different breath volumes prepares them to sing across styles, and with varying vocal intensity regardless of where they are in a breath cycle.

**Vocal Fold Function.** Vocal folds come together in a variety of ways—with thyroarytenoid (TA) dominant function (commonly described as Mode 1 or chest voice), or with cricothyroid (CT) dominant function (commonly described as Mode 2 or head voice.) In many Western classical genres, the goal is for the vocal folds to come together smoothly without any pressing or breathy air leakage. Conversely, some contemporary and global music styles have different aesthetic goals, including sudden shifts of function for a brassy belt or a breathy intimate sound. An instructor might direct students to semi-occluded vocal tract exercises or exploit a breathy blown tone for adjustment. Technological resources such as Voiceprint or VoceVista can also be tools for "seeing" vocal fold function.

**Resonator Shape.** Matching resonator shape to vocal style can improve the clarity of the vocal tone by directly impacting the vocal fold function. Is the resonator predominantly convergent (inverted megaphone) or divergent (megaphone)? Convergent shapes are typically found in Western classical and legitimate styles, while divergent resonator shapes are typically found in contemporary music theatre and some world music styles. Directing student/artists to the appropriate resonator shape can be done using a mirror or a helpful hand gesture. (Perhaps have them try placing a "C-shaped" hand alongside their own cheek as they sing, for a converted resonator shape, or placing the pointer finger toward the top of the nose and the ring finger toward the lips for a "sideways-V" or divergent megaphone shape.)

**Articulation.** As they say, those that speak well, sing well. Are the student's vowels and consonants balanced in length and line placement? How are diphthongs approached? Where are vowels "placed" in the mouth? How does the tongue act/interact with the jaw? Directing the student/artist to explore the more rounded articulation of classical long vowels, or the squarer articulation and strong consonants of music theatre, can impact the vocal quality.

"Taking stock" of the voice through the assessment framework suggested in this recipe can be a formidable tool in becoming a seasoned voice instructor. Using a discriminating oral/aural palate, the voice instructor can demonstrate, provide anatomical descriptions, recorded models, descriptions, and imagery to assist the student/artist. Sharing assessment with the student/artist helps them take ownership of their own artistry, reinforcing the methodology of discriminating listening.

Assessment informs our actions and is the first step in setting SMART goals—goals that are specific, measurable, actionable, realistic, and time-bound. Using this assessment framework, teacher and student/artists can "take stock" of progress and focus deliberately on specific tasks and holistic vocal development.

RECIPE

# Swinging Lasagna

*Kate Paradise*

When something swings hard, it *feels* good. Music that swings inspires people to dance and move in a way that feels natural, organic, and easy. However, performing music that swings requires much technical skill. Commercial vocalists and choirs, particularly those that work in jazz, blues, or hip-hop genres encounter swing subdivision frequently and benefit from practice in the art of swinging.

**INGREDIENTS:**
A metronome

**SERVES:**
All ages.

**Preparation:** Have students perform the following steps:

1. **Triplet Subdivision:**
   In written music, eighth notes always LOOK the same, but how they SOUND when swung is vastly different. When interpreting the melody of a swing tune, eighth notes are not created equally. Instead of each eighth note receiving half of the beat, the first eighth note receives 2/3 of the beat and the second eighth note receives 1/3 of the beat.

   ♫ = ♬♬ vs ♫ = 3

   How to practice this…
   - Put a metronome on at 90 bpm. Tap eighth note triplets on your lap, paying careful attention to keeping a steady, even tempo. Now speak swung eighth notes on the syllables "do-ba," lining the articulation of the consonants up with the first and third partial of the triplet.
   - Put a metronome on 110 bpm and walk around your classroom, stomping on each quarter note. Next, speak the word "merrily" on each beat. After about a minute, stop saying the second syllable of the word aloud. (Although, it helps if you continue to think it!) Practice adding claps on the "ly" syllable of "merrily" to feel where the offbeat occurs in swung feel.

2. **The Pulse:**
   When you perform in a swing style, quarter notes should be separated, and extra attention should be given to emphasizing beats 2 and 4.

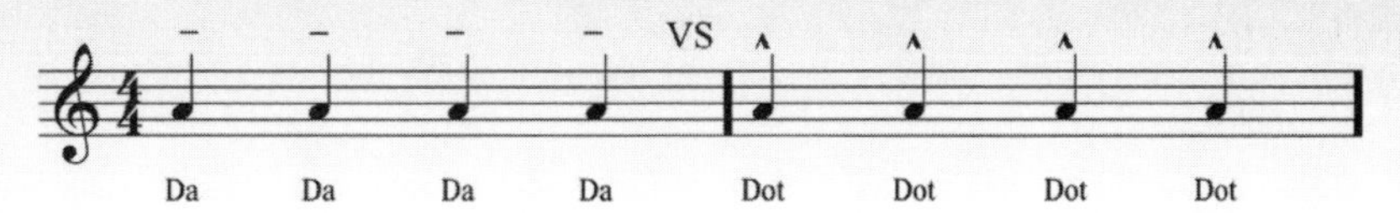


   How to practice this…
   - Put a metronome on at 120 bpm. Speak quarter notes on the syllable "dot," aiming to create space between each note without making them too staccato. In swing music, quarter notes should be "fat" and percussive. Now add a snap or clap on beats 2 and 4!

3. **Accents:**
   How you accent the notes within a melodic line can either emphasize the music's feeling of swing or deemphasize it. This becomes particularly important as tempos get faster and/or when singing in more instrumentally-driven styles of jazz, like bebop. Two great places for accents are on eighth note anticipations and on eighth notes that occur on the offbeat followed by a rest.

   How to practice this…
   - Listening for the jazz "flavor" articulated by great jazz singers and horn players when they take improvised solos! Learn a few of these solos and sing along. For example, Sonny Rollins and Clifford Brown on "Pent-Up House," Cannonball Adderley and Miles Davis on "Freddie Freeloader," Ella Fitzgerald on "In a Mellow Tone, and Sarah Vaughan on "Autumn Leaves."
   - Put a metronome on at the tempo of a song you are practicing. Snap on 2 and 4. Now "speak swing" the lyrics percussively, as if they are scat syllables. Play with using accents to emphasize the swing feel AND the natural rhythm and prosody of the language.

Assemble by layering the above components and bake. Serve with a garnish of light vocal tone. Pairs well with a count-off Chianti!

RECIPE

# Baking a Great Belting Sound

*Lisa Popeil*

You know you want to learn how to make this exciting sound, but perhaps you have been afraid to try? What if there were easy-to-learn techniques, which provided you, your students, or your choir safe ways to create a modern, expressive, even beautiful belting sound? Preheat your oven for the recipe below.

**INGREDIENTS:**
Posture
Support
Belter's Bite
Chest voice
Breath-holding
Resonance

**SERVES:**
Pop, rock, gospel and musical theater performers, show choir directors, and classical singers interested in expanding their vocal vocabulary.

## Directions:

1. Lift sternum so that chest is lifted and comfortably high while singing.
2. Expand side and back ribs and maintain this position while singing.
3. Lengthen back of neck, keeping head in line with spine.
4. Tilt head up slightly and raise the chin up a bit.
5. Do "Belter's Bite": a.) place pinkie fingers (5th fingers) between back molars and bite down gently; b.) feel chewing muscle engage on sides of face in front of ears; c.) remove fingers; d.) relax tongue in mouth with tongue tip resting against bottom teeth; e.) smile slightly with no lower teeth showing; f.) chin should protrude

slightly; g.) check for jaw flexibility by moving chin up and down, quickly saying "yah, yah, yah, yah, yah." Lower jaw should remain firm but flexible.

6. **Precise support:**
   a. **Upper belly:** Find upper belly "magic spot" with 2–3 fingers by making a loud "shh" sound and see which spot firms outward the most. Students should find their "magic spot" a 1/2 inch to 4 inches below their sternum (breastbone). This spot should be firmed OUT for every note they sing, (even for softer sounds and last notes of phrases), then relax it for breathing. Belting requires greater pressure in the airstream than singing in head voice and the "magic spot" is a key pressure controller.
   b. **Lower belly:** Place a thumb on navel and the rest of same hand below the navel on the lower belly. The lower belly should gradually clutch straight in for each phrase of singing, then relax completely for breathing.
7. **Chest voice:** Belting can be described as singing in high chest voice, often produced with a loud and resonant sound. So, what's chest voice? A modern definition is to think of it as a "talky" or "yelly sound." Though chest voice is often loud, full and heavy, IT DOESN'T HAVE TO BE.[1] This vocal register is both a sound heard in speech or yelling as well as a vocal fold vibrational pattern. Singers don't have to feel vibrations in their actual chests to be singing in chest voice.
   Compared to head voice, chest voice exhibits thicker vocal folds, with "squarish" edges, becoming less square on higher pitches. Also in chest voice, the vocal folds are typically closed more than 50% of every vibration. This allows less air to seep through the folds compared to head voice.
8. **Hyoid pull:** At the crook of the neck, below the tongue and just above the voice-box lies a little curved bone called the hyoid bone (See "Belter's Bite" image in step 5). When chest voice is taken higher than typical speaking range, singers may feel this hyoid bone pulling forward. The "hyoid pull" can help produce a natural-sounding belt voice in the higher range with ease.
   To experience the hyoid pull, start by engaging the "Belter's Bite" with one index finger placed up against the hyoid bone. Then have singers project their voice across the room by saying "Yeah!" higher and higher in pitch; many should notice that the hyoid bone is pushing gently against the index finger. That's the "hyoid pull!"
9. **Breath-holding:** Singers should feel like they're holding their breath slightly as they sing higher in chest voice.
10. **Resonance—Ring & nasality:** Though belting traditionally implies loud and resonant singing, one can actually belt and control two resonances, ring and nasality, separately. Singers can remain in chest voice but still be able to shift timbres to produce a variety of colors as the style or character requires.
    To increase "ring" (high-pitched, piercing, metallic sound) in your voice, do "ick face" by pulling up slightly on the sides of your nose as though smelling something foul. To reduce ring, relax the area on the sides of your nose. To increase nasality (buzzy, lower-pitched resonance) drop your soft palate. To decrease nasality, raise your soft palate like at the beginning of a yawn.

---

1 Lisa Popeil, "The Multiplicity of Belting," *Journal of Singing* 64, (2007): 77–80. A revised 2015 article "The Multiplicity of Belting" is available upon request at lisapopeil@mac.com.

**For Best Results, Don't Overcook—Tips for Vocal Health:**

1. **Vocal folds too thick:** Belting should not be equated with constant, extreme loudness or singing with overly thick vocal folds. Experiment raising your pitch in chest voice by progressively thinning your vocal folds using the vowel "aa" as in "cat." This thinning will help enable you to raise your pitch safely and beautifully while remaining in chest voice.
2. **Volume control—Mix it up:** Remind singers to not always sing loudly. Just as if they're doing eight shows a week in a musical or touring in a rock show, have your singers vary volume to protect against vocal fold trauma.
3. **Don't squeeze vocal folds:** Singing loudly doesn't mean one should pinch, squeeze or press the vocal folds. Over time, this is sure to create tissue damage. Instead, increase support (see step 6) while reducing your volume slightly—that's the magic formula for safe, loud singing without pushing or pressing.

RECIPE

# Recipe for Aging Voices

*Kathy Kessler Price*

Aging singers (and aren't we all to various degrees?) worry that a day may come when they will no longer be able to sing in a manner that pleases both them and their audiences. Solo performers adjust repertoire as they mature, and choristers may find themselves needing to sing a different voice part over time. There are very specific actions that we can take to continue singing beautifully through our lifespan and serve our audiences with a beautiful offering. Here's a recipe—a plan—to insure we all enjoy this art form so precious to us for our lifetime.

## INGREDIENTS:

**Primary:**
Vocal folds
Laryngeal muscles (thyroarytenoid (TA), cricothyroid (CT), and others) and structure
Lungs and respiratory muscles
Skeletal structure
Hormone replacement, if possible

**Secondary:**
Daily, short, focused 10- to 15-minute practice sessions (at least 2 a day)
A personal ENT with a voice specialty
Sleep
Water
Positive Attitude

## SERVES:

This recipe serves all singers, especially those who are in middle or older age. It also serves choral ensembles everywhere—those who are more and more filled with older singers who have leisure time and want to continue or resume their love of singing, and singing together. It serves conductors as they work with these singers. It serves audiences as they attend concerts, operas, and recitals—eager to hear music presented in ways that reflect the beauty of the music and the singer, colored by the beauty of age, but not impeded by its restrictions.

## Directions:

1. Prep time (warm-up and technical exercises) for the voice is 10–15 minutes of practice at least twice a day. These sessions are your personal practice time, in addition to any rehearsals. Long practice/rehearsal sessions are tiring and counterproductive, necessitating a recovery period following. It is important for conductors to under-

stand, as well, that mixing singing and non-singing activities throughout a 2-hour rehearsal is very helpful to the older singer. Constant singing in a lengthy rehearsal produces tired voices with improper muscle memory.

2. Begin with hydration. Water needs to be consumed 24 hours before active voice use to keep the mucosa lubricated and happy. Since you will plan to sing every day, increase your fluid (non-caffeinated, non-alcoholic) intake as much as is comfortable for you.
3. Sleep repairs and restores. Be sure to sleep at least 7 hours a night before active voice use.
4. During early middle age (somewhere between 40–50 years), a daily regimen of practice must be established and continued through the lifespan. The voice has begun to feel the effects of the loss of hormones, and therefore, the muscles must be exercised *daily* for elasticity and strength.
5. As we age, the chest wall becomes less compliant. Exercise your breathing through vocal exercises and daily singing, but also give yourself permission to breathe more often when necessary.
6. When vocal troubles arise, have a trusted voice-specialist on hand to contact (ENT with a voice specialty) to help you traverse the issues. Voice teachers and coaches are also indispensable. Be sure they listen to YOU—your concerns and descriptions of what is going on with your voice!
7. More trouble-shooting:
   a. If your problem is a weak voice, loss of strength and the ability to sing *forte*, your TA muscles need a workout! Be sure to exercise your chest voice with "ga," "go," or "gæ" syllables, singing sustained single pitches and 5-note, ascending/descending scales.
   b. If your problem is a strident, shrill, and inflexible voice, then your CT muscles need a workout! Start top-down exercises that begin in head or falsetto voice(s) and use [u] or [o] or [i] vowels to prompt a lighter-feeling, "heady" voice quality.
8. Flexibility/agility is necessary for singing, and if your voice is reluctant to move, then move it you must. Scales, descending triplet patterns, and ornamental figures can be practiced throughout the range, increasing speed as you improve.
9. Good overall physical condition is important as well! Participate in some activity that exercises the whole body system, and remember that such culprits as stiffness and arthritis have likely crept into our joints. Since the body houses and produces the singing voice, we must give it attention to stay strong and flexible. Whole-body exercise, however, does *not* replace vocal exercise, or vice versa. Additionally, mix standing, sitting, and moving about in rehearsals and practice sessions. Stiffness is an enemy to the voice, and if one is stiff in the body, the voice will eventually respond similarly.
10. If your health and family history permits, hormone replacement therapy can be very helpful. The voice responds to hormones, and as we lose them, we may lose range, stamina, dynamic control, and flexibility. Replacing hormones can be a bit of a fountain of youth, but not everyone can do so healthfully. Be sure to consult a medical professional for what regimen is best for you.
11. In singing, a "can-do" attitude is an essential ingredient. Approach singing with eagerness, joy, and a good work ethic, but don't overdo. In older age, over-practicing is detrimental. Sing smart. Listen, think through passages, practice down an octave, and stop a particular session before you are vocally fatigued. Come back later and try singing again after a period of rest.

Enjoy! ⊸

RECIPE

# A Recipe for Jazz Voice quality

*Kate Reid*

This recipe presents singers with tips and ideas for producing an authentic vocal sound for the performance of jazz tunes or literature in a jazz style.

**INGREDIENTS:**
The Vocal Process
Melodic Range
Speaking Register
Soft Palate
Resonance
Vowel Shapes
Diffused Tone
Vibrato

**SERVES:**
Singers of all ages.

**Preparing your ingredients:**

- **The Vocal Process.** No matter the style, the vocal process includes an initial inhalation and exhalation of air towards the vocal folds by coordinated action of the diaphragm, abdominal muscles, chest muscles and rib cage. The desired vocal tone will be a healthy sound and efficiently produced with the proper consideration of breath, breath management and resonance. The vocal quality of the jazz sound will differ from other vocal styles in timbre and color when mixed in with other ingredients in this recipe.
- **Melodic Range.** When choosing jazz material for vocalists, it is important to be aware of the technical facility of the student. In basic terms, their capability in shifting registers, or moving be-tween the speaking register and the head voice, will provide the foundation for success with jazz material containing a wide range in the melody. Younger or beginning students who are still working on and learning how to navigate between the various areas of the voice will be better served by jazz pieces that contain a smaller melodic range.
- **Speaking Register.** Jazz material containing lyrics is most often set in the speaking register of the vocalist's range; allowing the performer to deliver the melody and lyric in a conversational manner. In order to accommodate the individual voice and specific needs of any vocalist performing jazz material, the key of the tune or song, should be changed to fit the vocalist, better serve the lyrics, and ultimately

the story. (It should be noted that a great deal of jazz material and literature exists that is useful in building solid vocal technique and technical facility between the vocal registers.)

- **Soft Palate.** Often when singing jazz material, because of the conversational nature or the "sing it like we say it" presentation, the soft palate is not as raised or lifted compared to other vocal styles. However, it is this chef's view that solid vocal technique resulting in a healthy and properly produced tone is paramount. Therefore, in order to accommodate the melody appropriately, and sing healthfully in the extreme areas of the voice, the soft palate may need to be lifted more than we would in speech.
- **Resonance.** The understanding of resonance and its use is vital for vocalists in all styles. In a jazz context, the natural sound and resonance in the speaking register of the vocalist is desired. In some instances, a vocalist's natural speech may have too much of a nasal quality than is desired, and therefore consideration of less resonance when singing is an option.
- **Vowel Shapes.** More lateral vowel shapes that are closer to that of conversational speech are desired. Where some vocal styles require "tall" vowel shapes like "ah" or "aw," in words like "high" or "night," jazz vocal quality and style requires these words to be sung as they are spoken with the diphthong in "high" sounding like "eye."
- **Diffused Tone.** Many myths exist about the amount of breathiness in a jazz vocal quality. A diffused tone, or breathy sound, is typically undesirable unless used for an effect; i.e., facilitating a mood or the telling of the story.
- **Vibrato.** Vibrato is another coloring tool, like diffusion of the tone, available to the jazz vocalist. Vibrato used in jazz style is generally slower in speed than other vocal styles. Vocalists can use various widths of vibrato as well, i.e., an interval of minor or major second. Vibrato is not constant or immediate, but rather added toward the end of a note. Straight-tone, or the absence of vibrato, is much more common in this style.

**Step 1: Listening**
It is helpful to have a "sonic model" when singers begin to develop their own tone and style in jazz. Have singers consider all of the ingredients in this recipe when listening to jazz artists and stylists. Some examples include Carmen McRae, Sarah Vaughan, Ella Fitzgerald, Mark Murphy, Frank Sinatra, Tierney Sutton, Karrin Allyson, Nancy King, Gregory Porter, and Cecile McLorin Salvant. Listening in this way can be very helpful in developing one's own vocal sound and style in the jazz genre.

**Step 2: Mix Ingredients**
Combine various amounts and portions of the ingredients to find your authentic and genuine vocal sound for singing jazz music. Practice, experiment, and try different things to determine what comes easy and naturally to you. Enjoy!

RECIPE

# Original Recipes: Application of Vocal Technique to Address Artistic Choices in Original Music

*Kat Reinhert*

When working with songwriters who are taking voice lessons and bringing in their original material, there's no template from which to work. They are the composer and the performer. There may be an idea of what the songwriter wants the song to emote, and there's certainly an emotion behind the creation of the work, however, there's often a disconnect between what the emotion and lyrics imply and what's portrayed in performance. One way to help songwriters discover how to portray these emotions and lyrics effectively is by connecting vocal technique to sonic and emotional expression.

**INGREDIENTS:**
Emotional Map
Original Music
Song Crafting
Self-Accompaniment
Vocal Technique

**SERVES:**
Voice teachers in popular music programs working with original music; songwriters, students working on how to sing their original music; anyone working with artistic vocal expression; students in assessing their own progress.

In many voice lessons, students usually study music written and performed by someone else that they are inspired to learn. These pre-existing recordings and performances contain a template through which the student and the voice teacher can make sense of the material. Items such as vocal quality, range, registration and resonance can all be discussed, imitated, and finessed so as to accurately match the attitude and inflections of the original template.

However, what do you do when there isn't any template? Or when the template is being created as the song is being written, learned, practiced, recorded, and performed? How can voice teachers help their students effectively use their knowledge of vocal technique to address *how* they sing their original songs?

First, you need to address emotions. We all experience emotions. Songwriters are creating songs and there is an inherent understanding that they are feeling what they are creating. Addressing the disconnect between what they are feeling and how to portray that emotion is often challenging. Exploring and discussing the connection between the emotions and the voice is a good starting point. They can begin imitating certain expressions and emotions that occur in daily life. Then, through listening to and imitating recordings, they can learn how to reproduce these sounds that effectively portray specific emotions in songs. All of these emotions overlap with vocal technique, but often through this simpler exploration of sound, there is less fear about the discovery and creation of what some might call "strange" or "bad" sounds, thus freeing the singer to explore.

Then, through the application of vocal technique, a further and more in-depth exploration can occur. There are many different ways of discussing technique and many different methodologies for teaching it. What I'm talking about here is universal to all voice teaching—HOW to make sound. How does the voice make a bright sound? A dark sound? A loud sound? A breathy sound? A soft sound? Can the voice make all of the sounds that express the human emotional experience in all the different registers? If they can't make a certain sound, they can't express that emotion in a song, regardless of how much they *feel* the emotion. If they want to sing the anger that occurs when "my love has left me and I'm wailing," they need loud, angry, "nasty" sounds—and if they want to sing soft lullabies they need access to soft, breathy soothing tones. Learning how to make these sounds through technical exercises across the vocal spectrum and range can help to increase the emotive power of the voice.

Lastly, students can combine these two practices—emotional and technical—to create a template for the songwriter's original song. At first, this process will be slow and can be painstaking, taking each phrase, or sometimes each word, and discussing how to sing it. Is it a breathy sound? A loud sound? Should it be sung in chest or in head? Which register portrays the emotion that the song dictates? As this process is repeated, the body and brain can start to have a clearer understanding of how to quickly access these sounds. It also becomes more natural for the songwriter to think less about *how* and just *do*. This is artistry—where technical skill and the ability to convey feeling and emotional depth occur. It's where the *magic* happens—where they will create the template for others to follow.

# Soul Ingredients™: Onsets in African American Folk-Based Music

*Trineice Robinson-Martin*

Folk-based music styles within African American music genres represent musical extensions of black cultural expressions. The tones used, and the approach to singing, are direct extensions of emotional, animated speech; colloquial expressions; and regional dialects. To really understand a singer's use and approach to the various sound and style characteristics found in African American folk-based music styles, one must understand the culture the music represents, and the function music has as a cultural expression.

Many components of the tone or phrase contribute to how a sound is stylistically and emotionally perceived within the African American music culture. Each component includes a number of variations and approaches. Due to both the individualized and improvisatory nature of music interpretation in this culture, the emotional perspective of the singer determines the manner in which each variation is used.

This recipe focuses on onsets, and will describe some of the most prominent variations used in musical interpretation; as related to emotional perspective/context.

**INGREDIENTS:**
Onset
Delaying Stylistic Effects
Emotional Context and Perspective
Emotional Expression
Listening Examples

**SERVES:**
All Singers.

The start of a tone is called the onset. In folk-based African American music styles, the stylistic approach to an onset has both physiological and musical components. The manner in which these two components are combined contributes to how the emotion is perceived.

**Onsets—Physiological Variations:**
From a physiological perspective, there are four main types of onsets: hard onset, breathy onset, balanced onset, and "gravel" onset.

1. A hard onset occurs when the vocal folds are firmly pressed together and air pressure builds up underneath the vocal folds creating a harsh, pressurized start to the sound.

This sound, and type of onset, is generally used to create an accent when the word or expressive phoneme (i.e., a sign or moan) is a vowel sound. Emotionally, a hard onset tends to be used in moments of aggression, conviction, authority, or high emotional intensity.

2. A breathy onset occurs when an audible breathy sound starts before the vocal folds close/vibrate. In other words, an /h/ sound is heard just before the intended tone. This type of onset is generally used to create a light and gentle approach to a sounding a word or phrase. Emotionally, a singer can choose a breathy onset to create a sense of ease, nurture, and sensuality.
3. A balanced onset occurs when the start of the breath and the start of the tone are coordinated. The tone starts smoothly and there are no abrupt or breathy sounds added to the intended sound. Emotionally, a balanced onset can be used in absence of trying to convey a particular emotion at the start of the tone.
4. The gravel onset occurs when the tone starts as a vocal fry (i.e., a toneless popping sound) and then slides into a pitched tone. Singers use this type of onset when adding a squall or growl texture to the tone, and at moments of emotional exhaustions or emotional fury.

**Delaying Stylistic Effects:**
Physiological onsets are typically coupled with a stylistic effect. Regardless of the type of physiological onset used, the stylistic effect is almost always some sort of "delaying" musical effect as in a slur, slide, scoop, or crescendo. In other words, instead of producing the full, intended weight of a tone at the start of phonation, a delaying stylistic effect is inserted before the tone. The specific delaying effect used depends on the length and/or exaggeration required of the intended delay, which is ultimately determined by the emotional context. A small crescendo at the start of a tone is the most prevalent style of delaying effect. The crescendo can be perceived by the listener as "easing into the conversation" in a relaxing, colloquial, and conversational manner. Crescendos are most often executed on the same pitch as the intended primary tone.

Scoops, slides, and slurs are typically executed on a pitch below the intended primary tone. Using scoops is a quick way to accentuate the start of a tone, and enhance the rhythmic components of the groove. Scoops are the shortest delaying effect involving change in pitch, and typically not lower than a whole step below the intended note. Slides and slurs can be produced as much as an octave below the intended primary pitch, but are most commonly sounded a fourth below. Whether or not the first pitch, or the notes in between the first pitch and the intended primary pitch, is sounded varies between individual style preferences.

When a delaying effect is not used, the lack of use in itself *is* the stylistic effect. The silence or break before the start of the tone, often brings more attention and focus to the next sound, as it is often heard as a contrast to norm.

**Listening examples:**

1. "Cause I Love You" as sung by Lenny Williams.
   The song starts with the background singers and soloist using a breathy onset, with a crescendo effect. As the song continues, the soloist varies his onset choice between breathy, balanced, and hard onsets, depending upon the emotional context of the phrase. During the climatic moments of the song, one can hear the difference between the emotionally intense ad lib of a repeated "Oh, Oh, Oh, Oh." In the

first chorus, when "ohs" are accented, the soloist maintains a legato sound, creating a sense of vulnerability. As the song approaches a climax, the onset of the "oh" becomes hard, and the delaying affect is removed. This stylistic choice, from an emotional perspective, helps create a greater sense of emotional intensity and conviction.

2. "I Know I've Been Changed" as sung by LaShun Pace.
   Variation of a gravel onset and hard onset can be heard in LaShun Pace's rendition of the gospel classic, "I know I've been changed." The lyrics of the song is a simple declaration of one's state of being. Ms. Pace uses and maintains gravel and hard onsets, using various delaying effects throughout most of the song as if to emphasize the level of conviction and insistence of this definitive statement. The choir uses more of the balanced and sometimes breathy onsets combined with crescendos and slides. Emotionally this creates a soothing, and comforting contrast to the emotional soloist. It is synonymous to the dichotomy of emotionally erratic child, and the comforting voice of an empathic and compassionate parent.

African American folk-based music styles aim to musically express the emotional journey of what it *feels* like to be black in America. The music aims to both affect and effect performers and listeners to a collective sense of empathy, compassion, and community. Therefore, when singing and listening to folk-based African American music genres such as gospel, blues, soul, etc., one must recognize the approach to *how* a tone is sung and *how* a particular phrase is executed, is more significant than the tone and text itself. In other words, it's not *what* you say but *how* you say it.

RECIPE

# Staple Pantry Ingredients: Applying Exercise Physiology Principles When Training the Vocal Athlete

*Marci Rosenberg*

Voice production is a complex task requiring coordination of multiple structures simultaneously. Vocal athletes and professional voice users, such as teachers, are often at high risks for voice problems, given the extra demands on their voice production. Just as the professional athlete has coaches and trainers implementing exercise physiology principles to maximize performance and minimize injury, so too must the vocal athlete use warm-ups, cool-downs, and strengthening exercises to ensure career longevity and vocal health. Semi-occluded vocal tract exercises are an excellent way to promote vocal fitness.

**INGREDIENTS:**
Drinking straws
10 oz. paper cup

**SERVES:**
Any vocal athlete with high voice demands.
Any singer or teacher who experiences vocal fatigue.
Anyone who wants to preserve vocal health and wellness.

**What is a semi-occluded vocal tract (SOVT)?** This refers to any narrowing above the level of the vocal folds. Position of the tongue, palate, and lips can impose a narrowing or a constriction along the vocal tract.

**How does an SOVT improve vocal economy?** When completed correctly, SOVT's improve the efficiency of vocal fold vibration and the manner in which the vocal folds convert air pressure into soundwaves. When the acoustic pressure encounters a narrowing at any point along the vocal tract, some of that pressure travels back down toward the vocal folds creating a backpressure. This backpressure helps to reduce the amount of compression during vocal fold closure allowing for more efficient vibration and more resonant voice production.

**What are examples of SOVT's?**
There are many variations of SOVT exercises. In general, these recipes can be completed for several minutes at a time, multiple times during the day. SOVT's can be used as part of a vocal warm-up and as part of a vocal cool-down.

The following are four brief descriptions of SOVT recipe variations:

1. **Lip Trill/Raspberry:**
   Generate a lip trill first without voicing. Sometimes it is helpful to prop the sides of the cheeks up to facilitate this sound. Once this is established, add voicing in a gently gliding, siren-like manner. Start in your natural speaking range for several minutes until you feel maximum frontal vibration. Then move up and down in pitch maintaining the sensation of forward vibration. Once you ascend into your higher range (head voice), the frontal vibration will be less apparent. This exercise is also effective to improve breathing and airflow and allows one to easily go into head register.
2. **Straw Phonation:**
   This is one of the simplest variations of the SOVT exercises and is a great way to strengthen the voice. You can use varied diameters of straws depending on your response. Choose the diameter that provides you with the most sensation of forward vibration. This is often a drinking straw and this is typically a good initial choice. The straw is placed about two inches in the mouth. The singer is encouraged to sustain gentle, easy phonation in the form of glides through the straw, with no air leaking around the lips. Beginning in the speaking range, generate sound as if the straw weren't present; allowing for adequate airflow and volume. Emphasis should be placed on the sensation of vibration behind the front teeth and in the front of the face. It may take several minutes of practice before the singer settles into easy phonation through the straw. At this point, the singer can be encouraged to expand pitch range, however these are not meant to go particularly high. Explore with smaller diameter straws and strive to establish the same ease as with the larger diameter. One will often notice a nice calibration or forward placement of the voice after these exercises.
3. **Straw Phonation in Water:**
   In this exercise, the straw is submerged about a half inch into roughly 8 ounces of water. Follow the instructions from the previous recipe, Straw Phonation. The water has the added benefit of providing a visual cue to use airflow when producing sound. The deeper the straw sits in the water, the more the resistance. Play around with different levels of resistance when completing this exercise.
4. **Cup Phonation:**
   An 8- to 10-ounce paper or Styrofoam cup works best. Puncture a small hole about the diameter of a pencil on the flat bottom of the cup. Place the open portion of the cup around the mouth creating a complete seal.

Vocalize with a neutral vowel and glide up and down in a comfortable speaking range into the cup. Vary vowels and pitch range. Be sure that all of the sound is coming through the hole on the bottom of the cup. Resistance can be altered by decreasing or increasing the size of the hole. Emphasis in on forward vibration. This variation of an SOVT has the benefit of allowing for connected speech and singing.[1] When a cup isn't available, you can modify by using your hands to create a cup.[2]

SOVT's are an easy and efficient way to improve vocal economy and vocal fitness by improving the mechanics of vocal fold vibration. They are relatively easy to teach and execute making them a very useful tool for maintaining vocal fitness.

1 Marci Daniels Rosenberg and Wendy LeBorgne, *The Vocal Athlete: Application and Technique for the Hybrid Singer* (San Diego: Plural Publishing, 2014).

2 Alison Behrman and John Haskell, *Exercises for Voice Therapy*, 2nd ed. (San Diego: Plural Publishing, 2013).

RECIPE

# The "Pasta Dish" of Singing: The Essential Italian Ingredient, *Appoggio*

*Katharin Rundus*

Breath management is to beautiful singing as pasta is to an Italian meal; both must have a perfect balance of ingredients. In the case of *bel canto* singing this means a perfect balance of the singing muscles. This "dynamic equilibrium" enables singing that is freely produced, healthy, strong, and projects clearly into the room.

The Italian master teachers taught what has come to be known as the "*appoggio* method" of regulating the breath for singing. *Appoggiare* means to "lean against" or "support." Although this is widely used to mean that "the voice leans on the breath," another goal of the *appoggio* method is to create a muscular balance throughout the **entire body**. This helps stabilize the instrument for the aerodynamic forces that are necessary for beautiful, flexible, freely produced singing. Another way to think of this is that the muscles of inhalation and the muscles of exhalation agree to cooperate with each other to deliver a slow, steady stream of well-coordinated air to the vocal folds. This produces a consistent vibration that will be acted upon by the resonators and articulators to create beautiful singing.

**INGREDIENTS:**

A tension-free instrument (the body) that is in a state of muscle tonus, "ready to sing," including an open vocal tract.

A body (instrument) with hips, shoulders, ears aligned; the sternum is in a moderately high but flexible position.

Muscles of inhalation, the diaphragm and the external intercostals.

Muscles of exhalation, commonly grouped and called, "the abdominals" and the internal intercostals.

Constant cultivation, practice, and repetition to develop and maintain breath management.

**SERVES:**

The Singer; providing a long life of healthy singing.

Beautiful Singing; providing a perfect balance of breath and tone, perhaps the most important elements of the technique and art of singing.

The Audience; vibrant, energized singing contributes to the emotional experience and story telling our audiences crave.

The Soul, our metaphysical selves; well-managed breath that supports fully realized, beautiful singing enables humans to access the spiritual parts of their being—more than words alone.

There is a reason why in Latin, *spiritus* means both "breath" and "spirit."

Begin with your tension-free, well-aligned body and follow these four steps:

1. Completely exhale while maintaining the muscle tonus and alignment of your instrument. It is especially important that your sternum remains moderately high and flexible.
2. With your fingers monitoring your tenth rib on both sides of your body, robustly sniff in through your nose four times. You should feel your ribs moving your fingers away from the middle of your body; later this will become a deep, smooth inhalation. This is the "four-sniff position" and the position you will eventually maintain while singing.
3. With your ribs fully extended, side to side, pause momentarily, and then begin a sustained "sh" (IPA symbol [ʃ]) for exactly 4 beats. Do not allow your ribs to recoil back toward the center of your body while you are "[ʃ]-ing."
4. Then allow your ribs to recoil, and return to step 2.

Repeat these four steps with variations for further training.

- Always begin by fully exhaling.
- When you can fully expand your ribs side-to-side into the "four-sniff" position, substitute a deep, slow inhalation for the sniffing. Make sure your ribs are fully expanded.
- When 4 beats of "[ʃ]-ing" becomes easy without collapsing your rib cage, then go for 8 beats and then for 12 beats.
- Now still keeping your ribs stable for 12 beats, add a crescendo on beats 9, 10, 11, and 12.
- This is when the Italian magic begins. As you are experimenting with longer and longer "[ʃ]-ing" without your ribs recoiling, do you feel your abdominal muscles (muscles of exhalation) begin to engage and help maintain the side-to-side position of your ribs? This is the *appoggio* at work! Your inhalation muscles and your exhalation muscles are agreeing to cooperate to maintain the position of your rib cage, for a long as possible, so that you can send a slow, steady stream of air to your vocal folds for consistent vibration.
- Now instead of using [ʃ], sing "she" on a five-note scale. Can you keep your ribs expanded and your abdominal muscles engaged for the entire exercise?
- Repeat with longer and more complex musical phrases. As you are singing, notice that there is no undue tension in the core of your body. Just like the perfect Italian pasta dish with the right balance of sauce and noodles, you have created a perfect dynamic equilibrium in your muscles as they cooperate to maintain a steady breath flow by using the essential Italian ingredient, *APPOGGIO.*

RECIPE

# Soup to Nuts: Using Your Voice as Many Different Sounds

*Deke Sharon*

For most of human history, voices have played a rather singular role, primarily used to sing the melody and harmony with lyrics or neutral vowels, e.g., "ooh" or "ah," while instruments of all shapes, sizes, and sounds have been created and employed to support and fill out the texture. This has changed, especially within Contemporary a cappella, as singers from middle-school-age to empty nesters use their voice to create a modern "wall of sound," and imitate guitars, horns, synthesizers, and drums, or more generally, play the role of instruments and create an entirely new vocal "wall of sound."

**INGREDIENTS:**
A good ear
A pioneering spirit
Some great instrumental recordings as guidelines
Patience
A sense of humor (for the early stages)

**SERVES:**
The future of vocal music, as singers begin to explore beyond lyrics and simple vowels, learning to use the full timbral range of the human voice.

There is an exciting new world of sound to be explored by today's vocalists. Aside from pure imitation, there are many reasons a vocalist might want to sing like an instrument; e.g., to create more percussive or languid vocal texture or hybrid vocal-instrumental sounds (imagine scat singing somewhere between Ella's syllables and vocal trumpet).

Here is a recipe to help a singer move toward a more instrumental sound with their voice:

- **Stay away from words.**
  The human brain has a number of different regions in which specific intelligences are processed such as linguistic, kinesthetic, spatial, and mathematical. When we sing words or simple syllables like "doo" and "bop," our brain is processing the information in both the linguistic and music centers, and any listener can clearly identify the musical sound as coming from a human voice. If singers make a clearly non-linguistic sound, the brain will process it only in the music center, and search to categorize it within known sounds, which is how vocal percussion registers as, "Wow, you sound just like drums!"

One way to start down this path is to use syllables instead of words. "Dm," "bm," and "thm" all avoid an open vowel and make great bass syllables and sound more instrumental than "dum," "bum," or "thumb." If a vowel is needed, for more volume, make sure it doesn't combine with consonants to form a word ("thung," a nonsense word, will not distract the way "thumb" will).

- **Phrase like an instrument.**
  A vocalist's natural melodic instincts are informed by a lifetime of listening to singers. The natural use of glottal attacks on some notes and slides up to others are a dead giveaway to a listener that an instrumental part is being sung. Singers can break these habits and find new ways to phrase melodic lines by first imitating instrumentalists. Have singers listen to the way an instrumentalist's note is approached and attacked, the way it decays and resonates, the way vibrato is added, and so on. Some examples of great source material are trumpet solos by Miles Davis and Chet Baker, or YoYo Ma's solo cello recordings. Singers should memorize great instrumental solos and sing along to them, and focus on not only the notes but also the timbre and phrasing. In time, students will learn how to sing like an instrument, and can use these new-found instincts to approach melodic lines non-vocally.
- **Avoid diphthongs.**
  The sound of one vowel morphing into another, a diphthong, is a dead giveaway for a human voice, especially in English. Students should stick to clear, non-morphing vowels, unless they're making a sound in which it's essential (e.g., a trumpet with plunger mute, guitar with "wah" pedal, or flanging synthesizer).
- **Experiment.**
  Have singers find vowels that live in the cracks between the vowels used in everyday speech; listen to other languages to gather other uncommon linguistic sounds; develop a vocabulary of non-linguistic sounds; try imitating non-musical sounds to help them step outside of their natural vocal instincts. Be sure they keep track of these sounds to integrate them into compositions, arrangements, scat solos and the like.
- **Practice with the radio.**
  Most novice musicians sing along with the melody, yet more experienced singers sing along with the harmony parts, and advanced singers often create their own part. Contemporary a cappella singers become the band by beatboxing along, adding a guitar line, weaving a "Louis Armstrong-esque" trumpet solo throughout, and so on. Encourage singers to find ways for their voice to create a new sound or texture that complements the recording.

The human voice is the most powerful instrument in the world. Sure, a synthesizer can produce a wider range of timbres and pitches, but it can't make an audience laugh or cry within seconds. By pushing vocal boundaries, we're unlocking the potential for new sounds and styles of music, and the opportunity for vocalists to forge new paths beyond the melody. A couple of decades ago people scoffed at beatboxers and vocal percussionists, and now they're a significant element of hip hop and a cappella culture. What's next? That's up to you and your singers.

RECIPE

# Inclusive Pedagogy: Cooking in a Way that Feeds All Singers

*Stephen Sieck*

When working with singers, whether in private studio instruction or choral ensemble rehearsal, teachers need to remember that students are not all the same person, and therefore everyone in the room may need and expect different things. Teachers each bring a set of experiences and expectations based on our identities, which strongly influences the music we sing and the way we teach others. Inclusive pedagogy for singers starts with the idea that teachers want to teach every student well, and acknowledges that this means one size does not fit all.

**INGREDIENTS:**
Awareness of your identity, and that other identities may be different than yours
Compassion
Willingness to adapt your thoughts and behaviors

**SERVES:**
More singers than you ever knew you could serve!

**Recipe:**

1. Start with the assumption that every singer wants to feel empowered, respected, and valued. They might not show this, and may even act in such a way as to provoke your negative judgment. But this recipe works best if you believe that all singers deserve respect.
2. Next, set aside your pride to cool off in another room. This is about your student, not you.
3. Take as much time as you can to listen to each student. Don't just listen to their voice; listen to the stories, the experiences, the values, and the life of the person who offers that voice. In choir, this might mean taking more time in each audition to ask questions that start conversations, like "tell me about how music has been a part of *your* life," or "what do you like to do when you're not doing homework after school?" In voice lessons, this might mean conversations about how the student sees and understands their voice, and what they hope to share with others when they sing. Consider adding a "retreat" component to your studio or ensemble toward the beginning of the year that gives each singer the chance to express their values in a trusting and respectful environment.
4. When you select songs to sing, examine the context of the song in detail. Who is the poet, and who is the composer? To whom were they writing, and why? How

does this song fit within musical traditions that lift up or hold down some people? For example, with a little digging you can learn that in the 1840s, a white man composed the very popular American song *Oh Susannah* for white men to sing in a Blackface minstrel troupe.

5. You do not need to select songs that "match" your student, e.g., selecting only African American songs for a singer who identifies as African American. However, you should make your best effort to be aware of how the songs you select may affect different singers in different ways. For example, a song like *Oh Susannah*, which was part of a genre that mocked and oppressed African Americans in slavery, may feel deeply hurtful to an African American singer.
6. Whatever you select for your student(s) to sing, be prepared to talk about the music. We are all capable of singing songs that make us feel uncomfortable or fail to align with our own belief systems. Art doesn't have to comfort—it can also challenge. However, if we lead our students into such challenging moments without consideration, and without our own awareness of how and why it is challenging, we set our students up for conflict instead of learning.
7. As you teach, be attentive to the language you use. Be wary of adjectives and adverbs that promote inequalities ("girly" versus "manly," "educated" or "cultured" versus "country" or "urban," etc.), and focus instead on specific pedagogical instruction (fuller/thinner sound, taller/wider vowels, etc.).
8. Take a student's (dis)abilities and learning accommodations seriously. For example, if a student has a reading processing disorder, consider making a photocopy so that the student can highlight the lyrics to track the text more efficiently while singing.
9. It's okay that you don't know all of the sung repertoire of every culture in the history of the world—no one does. You probably know a small corner of it really well! Challenge yourself to find a few new songs every year that you were not taught, e.g., songs written by women, composers of color, composers from other nations besides Europe and America, or composers who observe religious traditions other than Christianity. You don't have to throw away the songs you are already expert in—keep those!—but take the time to expand your library of great songs to teach.

As you follow these instructions, continue your well-honed pedagogical strategies as usual. All singers need good alignment, breath support, laryngeal position, placement, diction, phrasing, and communication. This recipe should not affect those strategies, but instead works at a meta-level. By acknowledging the dynamics between, student and teacher, and repertoire and history, inclusive pedagogy helps to remove potential barriers so that the student's fullest attention is given to your pedagogical strategies for better singing.

RECIPE

# Transgender Singers Tetrazzini and/or Outside-the-Gender-Binary Bienville

*Loraine Sims*

These wonderful creations are made using an open mind, a willing heart, and the determination to encourage honest communication. Transgender or non-binary singer "casseroles" take a bit of extra effort, but the process is fulfilling and worthwhile.

**INGREDIENTS:**
An open mind
A loving spirit
A creative desire to teach any voice
Knowledge of fact-based voice pedagogy
Non-binary thinking
Non-heteronormative language
A safe space "kitchen"

**SERVES:**
Everyone.

Successful preparation of this "recipe" must include the desire to create a gender-neutral environment. Non-heteronormative language is a must. The savvy "cook" will recognize that gender and sex are not synonymous terms. Cisgender means that your assigned sex at birth is in agreement with your internal feeling about your own gender. Transgender means that there is disagreement between the sex you were assigned at birth and your internal gender identity. There is also a difference between your gender identity and your gender expression. Many other terms fall under the transgender umbrella: Non-binary, gender fluid, genderqueer, and agender for example. Remember that pronouns matter. Never assume. The best way to know what pronouns someone prefers for themselves is to ask. In addition to she/her/hers and he/him/his, it is perfectly acceptable to use they/them/their for a single individual if that is what they prefer. Some other pronouns are coming into use such as ze/hir/hirs, and may become more familiar with time.

Singers may or may not have a conflict between their gender expression and their singing voices. As you prepare these "casseroles," remember to check in often to see how the individual feels about the process. You should know that things often change and you may need to reevaluate how you continue working. Some individuals choose to take hormones and/or have surgery as part of their transition and some do not. A good cook knows that it is impolite to ask these questions. Honest communication comes after some time has passed and trust is established. Remember that your role as the "chef" involves you meeting the voice that is presented to you and working to help the singer achieve the goals that they set for themselves. A strong measure of reality may be added as needed, but always with a heaping cupful of kindness and respect.

Hormones have little if any effect on the voices of transwomen who use them. Therefore, it is possible for a transwoman to be a tenor or baritone if they wish. Some transwomen prefer to feminize the voice in both speech and singing. A speech language pathologist (SLP) may be needed to help with this transition. Simply raising the speaking pitch is not the only thing to consider. Inflection, intonation patterns, and resonance considerations are also important. Strengthening the falsetto is a must for the transwoman who desires to sing in the mezzo or soprano range. One of my favorite exercises to help achieve a bit more clarity in a weak falsetto production is the "uh-oh" exercise. Say "uh-oh" in a soft high voice, in much the same way you would speak to a small child who has fallen down. Then incorporate this soft glottal onset into a sliding, descending 3-note triad (sol-mi-do) on "oh" after the initial "uh" staccato. Encourage a vibrant slide rather than a straight-tone slide.

When considering transgender men, it would be possible for a transman to be perfectly comfortable remaining a soprano or alto. By contrast, testosterone therapy will create a profound and permanent change to the voice. In addition to the other physical changes that will likely happen, such as facial hair growth, muscle mass gain, and fat redistribution, the voice will deepen and lower in pitch. This is because of the thickening of the vocal folds. The newly lowered voice can be trained in much the same way that you would train a cisgender man, with slight modifications. The primary thing to help the singer explore is a comfortably low, stable laryngeal position with appropriate vowel modifications into the upper range. Transgender men who have trained as sopranos or mezzos may not easily grasp closing vowels rather than opening vowels as the pitches ascend. I like using the "oo" vowel to encourage this behavior. Encourage not opening this vowel until as late as possible and then aim for the vowel in the word "book." If an individual is beyond adolescence, the size of the larynx and vocal tract will not change. There are procedures that can block hormones to prevent adolescence in transgender children, but much more study will need to be done on this topic.

Please remember that transition is an individual process and there may be some "dishes" that are never completely finished. It will in no way diminish your enjoyment of helping to create individual improvement with your transgender singers. Open communication goes a long way to help create mutual respect and in this way, you can say that this recipe serves everyone.

**Read More About It:**

There are six transgender articles that have recently appeared in NATS publications. The NATS *Journal of Singing* featured four articles in 2017: "Teaching Transgender Students" and "Teaching Lucas: A Transgender Singer's Vocal Journey from Soprano to Tenor" by Loraine Sims, and a two-part article by Brian Manternach with contributions from Michael Chipman, Ruth Rainero, and Caitlin Stave, "Teaching Transgender Singers. Part I: The Voice Teachers' Perspectives" and "Teaching Transgender Singers. Part II: The Singers' Perspectives." Nancy Bos's article, "Considerations for Teaching Transgender Singers in College Voice" appears on the NATS Vocapedia resource and Shelagh Davies's article, "Training the Transgender Singer: Finding the Voice Inside" in the NATS Inter Nos online publication. Books on the topic include two from Plural publishing: *Voice and*

*Communication Therapy for the Transgender/Transsexual Client: A Comprehensive Clinical Guide* by Richard K. Adler, Sandy Hirsch, and Michelle Mordaunt and a new book scheduled for release in 2018, *The Singing Teacher's Guide to Transgender Voices by* Liz Jackson Hearns and Brian Kremer. ⊸

RECIPE

# The Singer and Pianist Team: A Collaborative Casserole

*Linda J. Snyder*

Throughout their musical lives, solo singers will have a partner in performances: the collaborative pianist. This musical team is much like a marriage, where "two become one." This marriage is also a well-seasoned and well-prepared casserole, in which various ingredients are tossed, blended, and balanced by two different chefs to become one organic and delicious dish; i.e., the artistic performance. The purpose of this dish is for both music and text to be aurally consumed as one and delightfully relished by the audience. This "collaborative casserole" is a delicate but complex dish, one that requires and deserves careful preparation in the mixing, cooking, and satisfying presentation to guests.

**INGREDIENTS:**
All should be flexibly prepared and able to be blended well together.

**Primary:**
Two different sets of sensitive ears
Accurate, clear, and expressive delivery of lyrics and musical score
Breathing in tandem by both chefs
Precise tempos, researched and prepared well by the musical ensemble

**Supportive:**
Clear communication skills on the part of each chef
Coordinated phrasing
Listening for artistic balance: melodic line vs. harmony and texture
Subtle piano pedaling
Rehearsal and performance spaces and acoustics
Creative imagery, confidence, and honesty

**SERVES:**
Efficient rehearsals.
A strong ensemble performance.
The lyricist's words and the composer's music, and the overall interpretation.
A performance fulfilling and inspiring for performers and gourmet listeners alike.

**Recipe Directions:**

1. **Prepare primary ingredients.**
   First, attend to the "4 T's of Preparation": text, translation (if in foreign language), tempo, and technology. Before rehearsing the music, direct the creative team to

research the text for clear understanding, purpose, and interpretation. This should be a "best practice" for both chefs. If the text is in a foreign language, the singer should provide a "word-for-word" translation. Ask your student chefs to practice performing *meaningful* words and phrases, not just syllables and pitches, in order to create a wonderfully expressive sauce from which all other ingredients will easily flow. Recommend studying multiple, tasteful performances of the music by means of today's technological resource, i.e., recording and accompaniment apps. Determine tempos, phrasing, and dynamic ingredients in delivering together the collaborative casserole.

2. **Add the supportive ingredients into the rehearsal mix.**
   As Martin Katz states in his book, *The Complete Collaborator: the Pianist as Partner*, "The primary building block of successful collaboration is surely the breath."[1] The singer is a wind instrument and must communicate the places for breathing and phrasing to the pianist by marking them in the score. A large measure of communication and a spirit of cooperation on the part of both chefs promote efficiency of rehearsal time, a sense of ensemble, and a smooth blend of all ingredients. To create the casserole recipe in rehearsal, layer the ingredients together one at a time, ideally in this order: text and translation, phrasing and breathing together, melodic line and rhythm, tempo and *rubato*, dynamics. To assess appropriate balance between the vocal and piano parts, add another dash of recording technology, or suggest a trusted peer listener. Try creative imagery in practice: ask the team to imagine presenting the casserole on stage; this may assist in preparing for inevitable distractions and in developing performance confidence. Recipe variations such as transposition or transcription adjustments of orchestral accompaniments should be agreed upon early in the rehearsal process.
3. **Blend and taste.**
   Have the artistic team stir together all the ingredients as long as necessary, so these will feel comfortably well blended. Add a portion of positive and honest critique. Based on this feedback and from that of a rehearsal video recording, explore seasonings related to pedaling, balance, intonation, natural expression and appropriate gestures. Consider possible recipe variations such as the team rehearsing in the performance space. Direct the pianist to consider options for difficult page turns, i.e., using a page-turner or preparing the original score (paper or iPad) appropriately so the keyboard may contribute fully to a smooth and supportive sauce.
4. **Bake and present.**
   Place the collaborative casserole in the pre-heated oven on the stage of the performance space. Direct the performance team to graciously acknowledge the warm applause and present the well-prepared casserole for the artistic and emotional satisfaction of everyone—including the chefs!

---

1 Martin Katz, *The Complete Collaborator: The Pianist as Partner* (NY: Oxford University Press, 2009), 7.

RECIPE

# Everything is a Mix: It Depends on Your Recipe!

*Kimberly Steinhauer*

The audition post called for "Belters with a strong *Mix*." The director asked the tenors for a "*Mix* in measures 8 through 16." The voice teacher preferred a "*Mix* instead of a *Belt*" to ensure vocal health. What is this thing called "Mix?" As usual, the voice mix depends upon the ear of the beholder. However, the Estill Voice Model proposes that each voice quality is a specific mix of anatomy and physiology that can be positioned, produced, and practiced by anyone!

**INGREDIENTS:**
Power Supply (Lungs)
Source (True Vocal Folds)
Filter (Vocal Tract Structures and Spaces)
Auditory Feedback (Ears)
Visual Feedback (Eyes to view the singer and the acoustic voiceprint on a spectrogram)
Control Center (Brain)

**SERVES:**
Anyone who speaks, sings, coaches, directs or conducts!
Anyone with a voice!

"Mix" can be defined as tone, timbre, or voice quality. But, what is voice quality? Jo Estill explained, "The voice quality of interest is the voice quality which remains after frequency changes, intensity changes, and vowel shifts are excluded. It is the voice quality that results from the manipulation of the larynx and the pharynx. It is the ambient quality of voice, the "ground" as we might say in music, that enveloping sound common to all vowels, and usually preset before any vowel is made. In water colors, it would be the basic wash of color, applied before any other detail or color is applied."[1]

The Estill Voice Model is a "Rosetta Stone" that translates the sound of a "Mix" into the corresponding physical movements of the voice box. When actors, singers, directors, and teachers speak the same language, the sound choices are endless and achievable. If this model describes "how the voice works," then Estill Voice Training (EVT™) prescribes "how to work the voice." To increase range, strength, flexibility, and endurance, vocal athletes separate craft from musical artistry using targeted exercises for anatomic structures called EVT Figures for Voice™. Each of these 13 structures moves to produce changes in voice quality that can be heard, felt, and seen. With EVT, vocalists choose Figure option

1 Kimberly Steinhauer, Mary McDonald Klimek, and Jo Estill, *The Estill Voice Model: Theory and Translation* (Pittsburgh, PA: Estill Voice International, 2017),

ingredients that mix to produce a specific voice quality output. A performer possesses the vocal freedom to make artistic choices and meet the vocal demands in repertoire, from opera to pop to musical theatre.

Since the definitions of "Belt" and "Mix" vary widely among pedagogues and performers, the following recipes outline the ingredients and instructions for an Estill Belt and Twangy Cry Quality (often called "Mix"). In EVT, each Quality is operationalized on the basis of vocal anatomy and physiology and, unlike registers, are sung throughout the entire pitch range. The qualities are described with prompts and the corresponding auditory, visual, and bodily-kinesthetic feedback, i.e., what the vocalist will see, hear, and feel. Both Qualities are produced with a relaxed, most comfortable vocal effort at the level of the true folds and use less breath than expected. In EVT, the amount of breath changes with each voice quality mix and must always be allowed to free-vary.

**The EVT Belt Quality — Mixing Instructions:**
**Prompt:** Your favorite team just scored the winning goal! Shout a joyous "YAY!" or "Ay!" Note that your "natural" cheer pitch is medium-high in your range. Sustain your joyous yell, and:

- Plant the sides of your tongue high by the top molars as if you must hold your dentures up, and listen to the slurping inhalation of the small breath in your mouth.
- Silently laugh and raise your larynx in your throat space.
- Anchor your head, neck, and torso as if you were suddenly surprised.

**Auditory Feedback:** Belt mix sounds thick, rich, bright, brassy, and quite loud throughout the range.

**Visual Feedback:** The spectrogram, or audio voiceprint, represents the extreme loudness of the Belt Quality throughout the entire frequency range with increased intensity in the speech frequencies (440Hz and below) and in the frequencies representing "ring" in the voice (2000–4000 Hz).

**Bodily-Kinesthetic Feedback:** You will feel more energy in the palate, sides of neck, and torso than you will at the true vocal folds if you sustain your high-effort laugh as you Belt. Don't be alarmed if you tilt the chin up for a louder Belt Quality.

**The EVT Twangy Cry Quality — Mixing Instructions:**
**Prompt:** The cutest toddler just walked into the room giggling and you cry out with the sweetest "Oh, YOU!" Note that this expression is also at a medium-high pitch. To build this sound:

- Sustain the "you" while cackling like the twangiest witch.
- Then suddenly whimper or cry like a puppy, while holding the twang feeling inside.

**Auditory Feedback:** Twangy Cry Mix Quality can be substituted for a the EVT Belt Quality because this powerful, ringing sound results from a narrow epi-laryngeal space that can be produced with a thinner true vocal fold mass.

**Visual Feedback:** The spectrogram represents the clear, sweet power of the Cry Quality via no inter-harmonic noise and higher intensity in frequencies representing "ring" in the voice (2000–4000 Hz).

**Bodily-Kinesthetic Feedback:** You will feel a small space in your throat and mouth spaces, energy in your soft palate, and buzzing in your cheekbones. It's easier to sustain this powerful mix by barely opening your mouth using a relaxed, Mid Jaw position.

After you practice sustaining the prompts, sing descending scales and short song phrases to experiment with your new joyous Belt *Mix* or your ringing, whimpering Twangy Cry *Mix*. ⊸

RECIPE

# Teaching a Countertenor, not Baking a Soufflé

*Peter Thoresen*

Too often, voice teachers approach teaching a countertenor with the same trepidation as a novice baker having a cautious go at a soufflé. A teacher doesn't need to tiptoe around a countertenor in the studio, and should lean into the essence of the primary vocal task at hand—the art of the breath and how it relates to countertenors, and similarly, to *all* voice types. Soufflé is French past tense for breath, and the voice teacher, like the baker, should take comfort in that very familiar and comfortable word and concept: good food is good food and good breathing is good breathing—no matter the dish or voice part.

Strategic vocal preparation and execution are key to engendering vocal beauty and sustainability in all voice types. When it comes to teaching countertenors, the secret ingredient isn't so secret a—it's a healthy knowledge of anatomy and vocal pedagogy for all voice types. Like all voice types and resonance choices, a countertenor's voice teacher needs to be prepared to explain and help to facilitate a variety of healthy vocal colors, not unlike a baker preparing variations of a sweet or savory soufflé.

**INGREDIENTS:**
A fully integrated understanding of how any voice type sustainably produces a beautiful sound
Diverse teaching and performance repertoire for students
A spirit of inclusivity
A fully stocked rack of vowel modification strategies
Heaping scoops of confidence in the knowledge of your teaching abilities

**SERVES:**
The countertenor in the studio; future countertenors in the studio and those who become teachers; anyone interested in embracing the fact that a countertenor isn't a voice type to be approached with extreme caution.

Frequently, teachers stock their cupboards with far too much unnecessary concern when it comes to teaching countertenors. Happily, in recent years, this is far less prevalent as countertenors continue to be admitted more frequently into collegiate voice studios—*as countertenors*—and also onto university and conservatory voice faculties. Yet this problematic anxiety about teaching countertenors still exists in many studios and among members of collegiate audition panels.

A myth among many voice teachers is that countertenors are a *different animal* or are *in need of specialized training*. This is a problem. The misconception that the countertenor voice type is somehow alien from the other voice types in terms of anatomy and the common tenets of healthful vocal pedagogy is wrong. That is an untruth veiled in the usual novelty associated with the countertenor voice.

To ready your studio for a countertenor, it's imperative that you are well outfitted with appropriate vowel modification strategies as codified by Ralph Appelman, Berton Coffin, Richard Miller, and others. Here, it's critical that a voice teacher not misapply modifications, e.g., giving soprano vowel modifications to a baritone. For the countertenor or sopranist, analogous vowel modifications for mezzo-sopranos and sopranos will do the trick. A countertenor's teacher should use the same range classification recipe as they do with other students, determining the locations of the *passaggi*, observing natural timbre, as well as comfortable tessitura areas in each part of the individual countertenor's range. Teachers of countertenors do themselves a service when they acknowledge that there are range classifications within the voice type itself. This is similar to a teacher differentiating a lyric soprano from a coloratura. Each singer has their own unique anatomy, and the countertenor is no exception. Slight differences in the length of countertenors vocal folds will result in range diversity—the longer the folds, the lower the voice. While most teachers immediately think of countertenors as mezzo-sopranos in terms of range, a good rule of thumb is to think of them as individual singers with ranges similar to their mezzo-soprano *and their contralto, alto and soprano counterparts*.

It is potentially dangerous when a countertenor—or his teacher—feels that he's vocally unusual to the point that his vocal mechanism must also be unusual. A countertenor's anatomy isn't specialized—the lungs aren't in the knees, and his larynx isn't in his elbow. Yet, it's important to understand that there is a risk in persistent *falsetto* singing. Research reveals that the vocal folds don't fully approximate in a small area of the folds during *falsetto* singing. Because the countertenor sound is the result of reinforced *falsetto* singing, there is a risk that negotiating this small, yet critical glottal closure issue can cause vocal fatigue, subglottal pressure and high laryngeal placement. Yet countertenors *are falsettists*, singing persistently in reinforced *falsetto*, so they must be taught to make this negotiation in order to avoid these risks. Here a voice teacher is well advised to impart instruction rooted in sustainability as they would for any voice type, but to additionally recommend occasional vocalization down an octave, in the countertenor's other/lower voice. This is his chest voice, which he uses anyway for both speech and singing in the lower part of his range—not his *falsetto*. This type of alternation can help to alleviate the problem of subglottal pressure and restore a more neutral laryngeal position.

Once a voice teacher feels confident in the premise that good, healthy singing is good, healthy singing among both the commonly occurring voice types *and* the countertenor, it becomes much easier to proceed with important work of preparing all of the singers who enter the studio. An example of this is Richard Miller's definition and reminder that *vibrato* is a phenomenon of the schooled singing voice, resulting from proper coordination between the breath and phonatory mechanisms—resulting in dynamic balancing of airflow and vocal-fold approximation. This reminder should empower all teachers of singing to exercise their countertenor students—beginner or advanced—similarly to other voice types. A countertenor only needs to suppress his vibrato when he feels stylistically compelled to do so, but not for long stretches of music.

In terms of the unique sounds of countertenors, teachers will need to give extra attention to the neighborhood of the voice in which the countertenor transitions from chest voice to his characteristic reinforced *falsetto*—frequently around E4-F#4. For the beginners especially, here it's important to encourage them to crack and sing, and sing through the cracks, to better learn how to navigate this part of the range. Going outside of the bounds of beauty helps all singers to consistently get back to beauty more quickly.

To conclude this recipe, it's important to note that the well-prepared teacher should feel comfortable applying the same repertoire selection strategies as they would with other singers, and not limit their countertenors to just the very old or the very new.

RECIPE

# A Well-Stocked Kitchen: Resources for the Voice Studio

*Cynthia Vaughn*

A chef's kitchen has the freshest, organic ingredients, rarest spices, and top of the line appliances to ensure a memorable dining experience. But the local food truck serves just as many foodie fans on a much smaller budget. What is essential for your voice studio?

**INGREDIENTS:**
One eager voice teacher
A room relatively free from distractions
Piano (or digital keyboard)
Mirror
Chair
Bookshelf
Songbooks and/or digital sheet music
Pencils
Metronome (acoustic or digital)
Notebook (for lesson notes)
Music stand
Straws (for semi-occluded vocal tract exercises)
Recording device such as a smart phone (for recording lessons)
Professional membership (NATS, MTNA, JEN)

**SERVES:**
Teachers and students of all vocal styles and levels.

**CHEF'S KITCHEN INGREDIENTS:**
*Note: Expert chefs have spent a lifetime collecting recipes, ingredients, equipment, and kitchen gadgets. It is certainly not necessary for the new voice teacher to stock up on all of these items at one time. Add new ingredients as your budget allows and your cooking style adapts.*

- Microphone and PA system (particularly for teachers of pop, rock, jazz and other contemporary styles)
- Sound attenuation (acoustic panels, rugs, curtains)
- Sports equipment for alignment, balance and breathing (such as balance board, exercise ball, physical therapy resistance bands, yoga bolster)
- High-tech kitchen gadgets:
  - Computer with webcam

- High-speed internet
- Skype or Zoom video chat software for online lessons
- External microphones for computer or smart phone
- Quality headphones
- iPad, iPad Pro, or tablet with PDF reader such as ForScore for reading digital music (optional: Bluetooth foot pedal to turn pages)
- Classical vocal digital download sources: ClassicalVocalRep.com, everynote.com, IMSLP.org
- Pop, rock, music theater vocal digital download sources: MusicNotes.com, SheetMusicDirect.com, GuitarTabs.com
- Sheet music streaming service (monthly fee): SheetMusicDirect.com PASS subscription
- Studio management software: My Music Staff, Music Teachers Helper, Studio Helper, Fons, Acuity
- Social Media: Instagram, Facebook, LinkedIn

**Culinary School/Professional Development:**
Beginning chefs cook what they know and start with simple recipes. Beginning voice teachers teach what they know and start with basics. Eventually, most teachers have a desire for professional development and learning from mentors. Voice teachers are encouraged to attend professional conferences, summer workshops, and certification programs, such as

- NATS (National Association of Teachers of Singing): National conferences are held every two years in North America
- ICVT (International Congress of Voice Teachers): Conferences are held worldwide every two years, alternating with the NATS Conference
- MTNA (Music Teachers National Association): National conferences and state conferences are held annually
- Summer pedagogy programs: Contemporary Commercial Music Vocal Pedagogy Institute at Shenandoah University, Somatic Voice Work at Baldwin Wallace, Vocal Pedagogy Professional Workshop (VPPW) by Boston Conservatory at Berklee
- Certifications: Vocology, CoreSinging, Estill Voice Training, MTNA
- Blogs, podcasts, and webcasts: NATS Chats, Every Sing by Nancy Bos, Why We Sing by Erin Guinup, VoiceScienceWorks vocology blog
- Business courses to market your studio: Online courses, local small business association, Chamber of Commerce

Most importantly, voice teachers are encouraged to keep their own sense of play, curiosity and wonder of the human voice. If you are a young teacher, learn from master teachers and mentors. If you are an experienced teacher, remember what it was like to be a new voice teacher and an eager young student. Explore and savor new tastes and new music. The kitchen is open and singing is now served!

RECIPE

# Let's Talk about the Tongue: A Recipe for Improved Vocal Ease and Function

*Catherine A. Walker*

Any in-depth investigation of the tongue and its functionality will likely yield some surprises to even the most seasoned voice professional. Many articles and pedagogical texts discuss the importance of tongue position at great length but rarely explore the impact of its efficiency and freedom of movement on the vocal outcome. The tongue's movement and use patterns have a profound impact on both the singing and speaking voice. By its sheer size, the tongue dramatically impacts a singer's: tone quality; ease of production; volume; articulation; and clarity of diction.

**INGREDIENTS:**
1 Curious and committed vocalist
1 Mirror or video recording device
Preparation requires time, repetition & patience

**SERVES:**
These exercises will serve everyone who wishes to optimize vocal use for both singing and speaking!

You cannot fully appreciate the complexity of the tongue's function without a more in-depth understanding of its composition. The tongue consists of multiple groups of muscles, which are responsible for tasks such as swallowing, tasting, chewing, licking, and articulating speech. The tongue is controlled by intrinsic and extrinsic muscles acting in concert. The intrinsic muscles are composed of layers of muscle fibers that are described as transverse, longitudinal, and vertical. The extrinsic muscles function like an elaborate sling, cradling the visible part of the tongue and allowing it to move in a variety of directions. Due to the nature of the tongue structure, anything you do in one part of the tongue will affect all other parts of the tongue. Therefore, less than optimal function in any *one* of these muscles will affect the freedom and flexibility of the tongue and, consequently the voice, as whole. Through tongue release exercises, the tongue will soften and consume **more space** in the mouth. It will also rest softly against the hard palate. The following exercises encourage the tongue to articulate in new ways and help to release chronic tension patterns. Using a mirror or the video function on your phone while practicing any of these exercises, will help you become more conscious and aware of how you are actually using your tongue. By exploring new movement patterns, the voice will gain freedom and flexibility, which will become immediately noticeable.

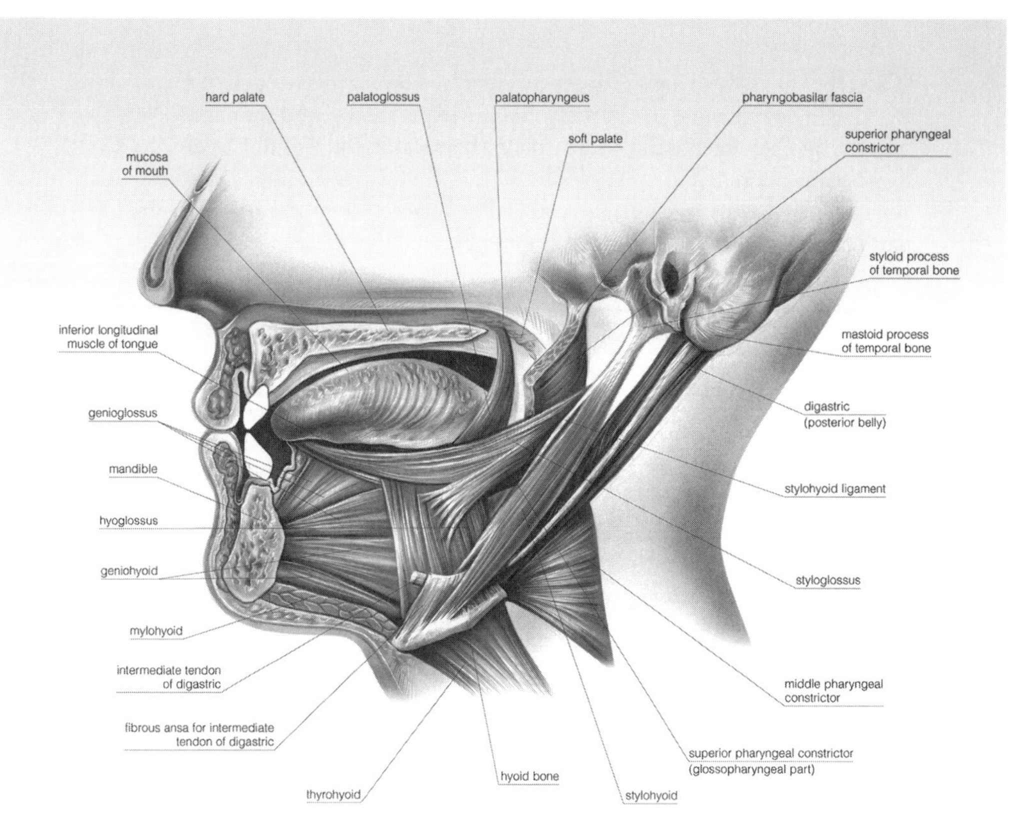


Used with permission and supplied by Science Source.

**These exercises activate the middle and back of the tongue, improve articulation, and diction clarity.**

1. Lightly touch the tip of the tongue to one corner of the mouth where the lips come together. Softly maintain contact of the tip to corner while slowly and deliberately articulating the text, using the middle and back of the tongue. Repeat this process on the other side.
   *Note: You may notice that speech or singing clarity differs from side to side. Although our bodies are bilaterally symmetrical, our patterns of use are rather asymmetrical. Look closely at your face in a mirror; you will see slight differences from side to side. The tongue is no exception. Through these exercises, you can "rebalance" your use patterns.*
2. Lightly touch the tip of the tongue to the anterior of the alveolar ridge (where your front teeth meet your hard palate). Softly maintain contact while slowly and deliberately articulating the text, using the middle and back of the tongue.

**These exercises activate the middle and back of the tongue. Releasing the muscles in the pharynx, dramatically affects tone quality and diction clarity.**

*Note: You will be releasing the pharynx in three areas: nasopharynx, oropharynx, and laryngopharynx. Remember that the posterior tongue creates the front wall of the pharynx.*

1. "Chewbacca": Create a uvular trill, much like the sound created by Chewbacca in the movie *Star Wars*, while articulating speech. Repeat, adding pitch.

2. "Cat Hiss" or "Daffy Duck": By gently creating closure in the back of the mouth as if you able to articulate the letter "k," you will create a sound similar to Daffy Duck or a cat hiss. Articulate the text through this sound. You will not be able to do this exercise on pitch.
3. "Gargle": By simulating a gargle, you will be able to access the tissues in the lowest part of the tongue as well as the sphincter created in the laryngopharynx. Articulate the text while gargling then repeat, adding pitch.

**These exercises assist in the general release of the entire complex.**

1. "Tongue Pull": Wrap gauze around the tongue. Gently pull it forward (out of the mouth). Hold for 20 seconds.
2. "Tongue Slide": Gently slide the tongue in and out of the mouth, letting it pass between the teeth and over the top of the lower lip. The tongue muscles should be soft and released, avoiding pointing or tensing the tongue.
3. "Tongue Glides": Slowly glide the tip of the tongue around the outside of your upper teeth from the far left to the far right. Repeat this on the outside of the lower teeth. Repeat this process again on the inside of your teeth.

The tongue is used for singing, speaking, chewing, swallowing and licking. Our chronic use patterns are repeated countless times throughout both day and night. Making substantive, long lasting changes to your tongue's use patterns will take time, repetition, daily practice and a great deal of patience. That being said, it takes time, but is possible. This kind of work is extremely impactful and will help optimize your vocal health and flexibility.

RECIPE

# Hearty Country Jam with Vocal Stylisms

*Edrie Means Weekly*

"Country Music—'Cause I'd rather listen to songs about trucks, beer and small towns than songs about what a fox says!" Anonymous

**INGREDIENTS:**
A country song
A singer
A good sense of Tennessee/country dialect, formation of vowels, diphthongs and triphthongs with a dash of twang
A flexible larynx
Capability of altering the shape of the vocal tract
Emotion and expression
*Optional: singer plays the guitar

**SERVES:**

The singer, the singing style, the musical style and the listener.

Vocal stylisms are to the singer as seasonings are to a great chef. They must include several different flavors to enhance overall taste. **Use caution and always aim for healthy functional singing while using the following vocal stylisms.

**Mixing Flavor Options for Vocal Stylisms:**

- Bend notes ("bending"/added blue note): a short slide from half step below.
- Add-on notes: similar to a pop appoggiatura, uses the prior note as the accent to the next note. It's usually a third or more higher/lower.
- Cry: adding a grace note from above, sounds like a whine
- Fall offs/ups: ending note slides down/up to no specific pitch
- Fry (creaky voice): loose glottal closure that creates a rattling or popping sound.
- Growls: a low, guttural sound produced with the false vocal folds and pharyngeal constriction.
- Flip onsets/Pop appoggiatura: an accented grace note from a half step below, often quick.
- Retracting tongue for dialect: the tongue is in a retracted position, i.e., [i] becomes [əi]; [u] becomes [əu].
- Licks: Brief improvisation; often a short phrase.
- Riffs/Wails: longer improvisational phrases mostly used in country pop.
- Slides (end slide-up, slide-down, fry slide): steady slide upward or downward.

- Swinging the note: straight eighth notes become a rhythm of a dotted-eighth-sixteenth couplet.
- Tails: three and five note descending patterns.
- Waves: pulsating on final note that includes several quick bent notes; mostly used in country pop.
- Yodel: intentional register shift from chest to head or falsetto.

**Instructions:**

1. **Finding the Song.** Pick a country song for your singers that is suitable for their voice and singing level. For starting out, have singers look at old country standards. A beginning voice student doesn't start off singing an aria, they begin with a simple art song.
2. **Vocal Tone.** The vocal tone is speech-based delivery, tending to be a Tennessee accent with a mixture of head, mix, chest, belt, and falsetto. The tone can be breathy at times especially in romantic ballads. Nasal resonance or "twang" is present in most country music—more so in bluegrass and less in romantic country songs. Country pop songs can have "belty" moments throughout with pop riffs. The vocal coloring may be dark or bright, and vibrato may be fast, delayed or straight tone.
3. **Finding American Twang.** If singers don't possess a natural American "twang" or southern country accent, refer them to *Acting with an Accent* written by dialect specialist David Allen Stern. These booklets span a variety of American accents including American Southern, Mid-West farm, and Texas. All booklets cover intonation, speech rhythm, muscularity/resonance, pronunciation and include IPA and a CD.
4. **Building Technique.** On a technical level, in order for the singer to be successful in country music, they will need to cross-train their vocal production muscles to create laryngeal flexibility. The singer can switch back and forth between registers by making different interior shapes to allow changes in the resonance to serve the style. Good country singers greatly vary their tone quality by altering the shape of the vocal tract, which extends from the true vocal folds to the mouth opening, and by adding "vocal stylisms" (a term I made up years ago to describe the extra nuances in Contemporary Commerical Music [CCM] and musical theatre) to support the style.
5. **Vocal Tract Shape.** The singer is in control of these physiological and acoustical changes involving movement of the jaw, tongue, and soft palate. Often the soft palate is dropped and the tongue retracted. In bluegrass or mountaineer songs the tongue pretty much remains retracted throughout. This tongue retraction can be attributed not only to the dialect/accent, but also, in the early days, to men trying to keep chewing tobacco in the sides of their mouth while singing. This retracted position could lead to more jaw/tongue tension, so be careful and do tongue stretches and exercises to loosen up after singing bluegrass. A good tongue isolation for flexibility exercise is "Guy-la," "Guy-La" (without moving jaw) on 5–4–3–2–1–2–3–4–5–4–3–2–1. Starting on G4 women, G3 men, going up the scale by half steps to D5 for women and D4 for men.
6. **Creating Expression.** Emotion and expression is created vocally by varying the dynamic, coloring the tone, varying the use of vowels and consonants, emphasizing alliterations and adding "vocal stylisms." (See Figure 1 and 2) The singer can shorten the vowel and emphasize a particular consonant or use "word painting" to color lyrics by creatively singing onomatopoetic words such as "chirp," "drip," "bang," "knock," "zip," and "click," as if to make them sound like the things the

words represent. On words such as fall and drool, it's also possible to seem to "fall off" the pitch by sliding down to the next note, which adds more color and emphasis to the meaning of the words. Learning "vocal stylisms" and functional vocal exercises can enhance stylistic skills and performance in country music.

Figure 1: Original Song Excerpt

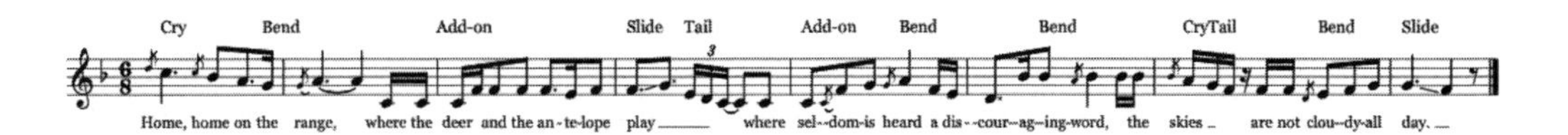


Figure 2: Added Vocal Stylisms

Enjoy a Hearty Country Jam, "Y'all come back now, y'a hear?"

RECIPE

# Serving the Students: Developing a *Mise en Place*

Brian J. Winnie

All repertoire is essentially a menu of various, authentic vocal recipes that are based in foundational ingredients, or "staples," of vocal production; i.e., components of breath, onset/tone, and resonance. To become a skilled chef, every teacher and student should become versed in vocal function, anatomy, and basic psychoacoustics (sound perception). This preparation includes the structures of the vocal mechanism (true vocal folds, false vocal folds, aryepiglottic sphincter, thyroid & cricoid cartilages, larynx, tongue, velum or soft palate, lips, jaw, breath, and alignment), their function, and the nonlinear relationship between ingredients; i.e., airflow can influence the true vocal folds, and true vocal fold changes can influence airflow.[1, 2]

By exploring and then labeling each component of the vocal mechanism, teachers and students can begin developing a common language based in voice science. This common language can better serve students in the voice studio and choral rehearsal, as well as curricula in vocal pedagogy, vocal diction, conducting, and choral methods. Once students become familiar with the ingredients of vocal production they can develop their *Mise en Place* for any vocal recipe.

**INGREDIENTS:**
Collaborative spirit
An understanding of vocal anatomy and function
Spectrum analyzer software or application
Diverse repertoire (menu building)

**SERVES:**
Voice teachers, choral teachers, classroom & methods teachers, and *most* of all, students!

In the word of master chef Jacques Pepin, "I tell a student that the most important class you can take is technique. A great chef is first a technician. If you are a jeweler, or a surgeon, or a cook, you have to know the trade in your hand You have to learn the process. You learn it through endless repetition until it belongs to you." Chefs must thoroughly understand their craft by studying the foundational elements of cooking and learn to prepare ingredients to efficiently complete any recipe. However, before starting a recipe,

1 Lynn Maxfield, Anil Palaparthi, and Ingo Titze, "New Evidence that Nonlinear Source-Filter Coupling Affects Harmonic Intensity and *fo* Stability During Instances of Harmonics Crossing Formants, *Journal of Voice* 32, no. 2 (2017): 149–156.

2 To dive further into this recipe consider attending an Estill Voice Training Course at www.estillvoice.com.

chefs gather the necessary ingredients and spend time preparing their *Mise en Place* for the menu. As a cooking technique, *Mise en Place* means "putting in place." Similarly, singers should have an understanding of the kitchen (body), the ingredients (anatomical structures), and amount (structural movement capabilities) of each ingredient to prepare their *Mise en Place* for any recipe the repertoire requires.

**Developing a *Mise en Place*:**

1. First, remove bias from the room. Some people don't like mushrooms and some don't like nasality, but some recipes are never the same without them. Start from the student's current vocal recipe (structural components and their relation to each other) and help them understand that a variety of sounds are needed for various qualities as long as they are executed in a healthy way. For example, a recipe used in the voice studio for classical repertoire will vary from one used in the choral rehearsal for an Indian raga. Help the student learn that both recipes are healthy and necessary for authentic, stylistic performance practices. Then explore the differences between the recipes to ease any confusion. With a common language, the choral director can succinctly state that a desired recipe incorporates a higher larynx position, thinner vocal folds, aryepiglottic narrowing, and a mid velum. The voice studio teacher then knows exactly what's being asked of the student and can help the student toward that recipe.
2. Develop a common language between teachers and students in regard to a student's vocal recipe without being afraid to use technical terminology. Instead of saying, "That was a tight sound," try saying, "That sound had false vocal fold constriction. Let's try an exercise to find a more retracted false vocal fold position." Teachers can accomplish this task by utilizing a vast array of exercises and approaches that fit the student's learning style. Labelling specifically the anatomical or acoustic goal helps the student incorporate that feedback in other classroom assignments with less chance of confusion.
3. Explore each ingredient of vocal production and the resulting changes in sound and sensation with each student; i.e., lowering the velum by breathing through the nose results in a nasalized sound and a sensation of sympathetic resonance in the "mask of the face."
4. Students should practice the movement capabilities of each vocal structure, independently of another, prior to completing a full recipe. Help them understand that a vowel can be altered by changes in tongue position independent of the vocal quality associated with the vowel.[3] For example, although [i] is heard as a "bright" vowel, we can make it sound "dark" without changing the tongue from its high position and instead lower the larynx. (Laryngeal position alters the resonating frequencies of the vocal tract; i.e., a raised larynx creates a shorter vocal tract and emphasizes higher resonating frequencies whereas a lowered larynx creates the opposite effect.) Develop vocalises and warm-ups that guide students through independence of tongue position from laryngeal position. Have students sing [ŋ] while subtlety changing the larynx position, and eventually change from [ŋ] to [i].
5. Increase the student's appetite for vocal quality recipes through teacher and self-guided listening sessions. In cooking, you have to experience the flavor to know how something tastes, likewise singers should experience recorded examples to develop their "vocal flavor palate."

---

3 Kimberly Steinhauer, Mary McDonald Klimek, and Jo Estill, *The Estill Voice Model: Theory and Translation* (Pittsburgh, PA: Estill Voice International, 2017), 12.

6. Augment vocal learning via spectrum analyzer software or acoustic applications. Spectrograms are visual representations of the frequency and intensity of a sound through time. This graphic representation can help students visually track changes in various components of vocal production; i.e., breath noise, onsets, vowel formants, and more. These tools can be helpful in both the voice studio and the choral classroom.
7. Translate metaphor or imagery into common anatomical language. For example, instructing the students to "direct the sound up and over, as if throwing a basketball," might achieve a "taller," "focused," or even louder sound. However, which outcome was intended by the exercise? Since metaphor can be misinterpreted easily, it's important to develop an exercise with a clear objective and then label the result. When students understand the objective (in this case, raising the velum) there will be a greater chance of reproducing the sound, and less confusion explaining their goals to another voice or choral teacher.

Through understanding the ingredients of vocal production and by developing a common language, students can develop their *Mise en Place* and alter recipes within multiple classroom settings with ease. The restaurant is open and every dish is welcome!

RECIPE

# Cooking Up a Recipe Full of Vocal Color

*Alan Zabriskie*

The goal of any voice teacher and singer is to develop a healthy vocal tone quality. This is best accomplished through helping individual singers achieve healthy vocal technique through proper alignment, breath, resonance, and placement.

**INGREDIENTS:**
Singers who are working to develop healthy vocal tone quality
Music of various styles and time periods
A spectrum of vocal color
Consistent instructional vocabulary

**SERVES:**
This recipe is designed to help singers in the solo and choral settings to develop healthy vocal technique, and variety of vocal color based on the *bel canto* concept of *chiaroscuro*.

In working to develop proper resonance and placement, the vocal pedagogy terms *chiaro* and *oscuro* can be utilized to help singers find a *chiaroscuro* balance that creates freedom and vibrancy.

1. *Chiaro* placement:
   In order to develop the *chiaro* (bright or forward) sound, the [n] consonant is utilized in conjunction with the [i] (as in "me") and [e] (as in "may") vowel sounds.

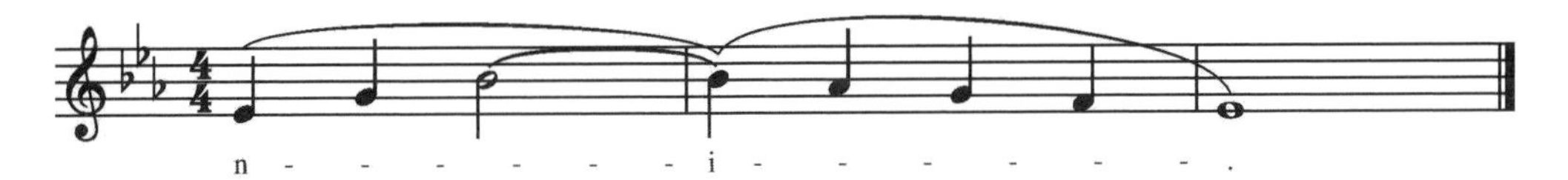


2. *Oscuro* placement:
   The *oscuro* (dark or round) tone quality is achieved through a [ŋ] (as in "sing") sound sung with the mouth open and through vowels [u] (as in "moon") and [o] (as in "note").

3. *Chiaroscuro* placement:
The balanced *chiaroscuro* sound is achieved by working for a somewhat centered placement of the sound while maintaining proper resonant space. A physical activity that is helpful in finding the proper balance is a placement meter:
The finger is placed at the side of the mouth and is directed toward the intended placement (i.e., forward for the *chiaro* placement, backward for the *oscuro* placement, and straight up for the *chiaroscuro* placement.
Once the proper sensation is achieved through utilization of the placement meter, the [hʌŋ] ("hung") syllable combined with the [a] (as on "h̲o̲t") vowel achieves the desired quality.

The mastery of placement of *chiaro*, *oscuro*, and the balanced *chiaroscuro* is an important aspect of the vocal technique of the singers for the alteration of tone quality, and can be instrumental in developing the singer's ability to create a spectrum of colors. Once healthy vocal technique is accomplished, the teacher can then work to develop a palette of colors and depth of sound to meet the demands of a wide variety of musical styles. In standard Western classical recipes, tone quality can be most healthfully altered by placing the sound towards five different resonance areas or "Resonance Factors."

**Resonance Factor 1:** The *chiaro* tone quality that employs full forward placement. This Resonance Factor is used when the brightest sound is desired.

**Resonance Factor 2:** Placement between *chiaro* and *chiaroscuro*. This Resonance Factor is used when the desired placement is forward, but not as bright as the *chiaro*.

**Resonance Factor 3:** The *chiaroscuro*, or balanced tone quality. This Resonance Factor is a balance of the *chiaro* and *oscuro* tone qualities.

**Resonance Factor 4:** Placement between *chiaroscuro* and *oscuro*. This Resonance Factor is used when the desired placement is backward, but not as dark as the *oscuro*.

**Resonance Factor 5:** The *oscuro* tone quality that employs full backward placement. This Resonance Factor is used when the darkest sound is desired.

When students are asked to produce the different resonance factors, they easily make the change with dramatic, healthy results especially through the use of the placement meter. In addition, utilization of an X/Y graph serves to specify the extent of lyric/dramatic and *chiaro/oscuro* for a given piece. Singers are able to make decisions regarding the stylistic characteristics of each piece and plot a point that indicates the desired placement (*chiaro/oscuro)* according to the above Fmentioned resonance factors, and the overall depth of sound (lyric/dramatic).

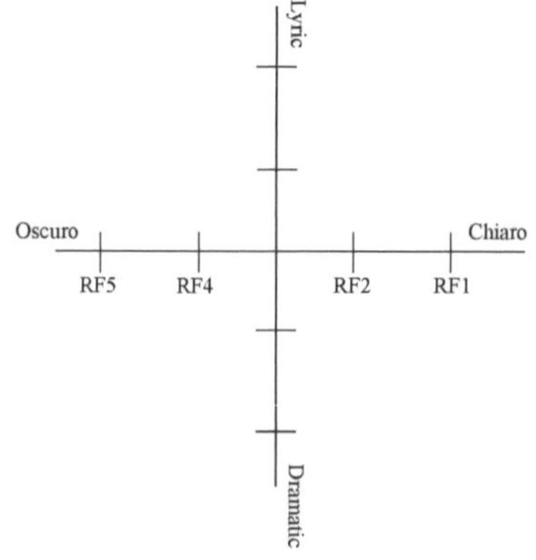

Any singer is capable of developing a wide spectrum of sounds and colors. The challenge is to accomplish this in a healthy manner that contributes to healthy vocal technique. Working to alter placement, resonant space, and depth of sound develops a sense of flexibility of tone quality in the voice of the singer in a healthy way that creates variety and interest for singer and audience. ⊸